MAGIC OR NOT?

Also by Edward Eager

Magic or Not?

EDWARD EAGER

Illustrated by N. M. Bodecker

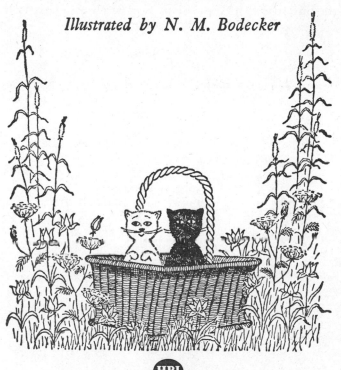

A Voyager/HBJ Book
Harcourt Brace Jovanovich, Publishers
San Diego   New York   London

Printed in the United States of America

The author and publisher thank Charles Scribner's Sons for
permission to quote lines from Edwin Arlington Robinson's poem
"The House on the Hill."

Library of Congress Cataloging in Publication Data
Eager, Edward McMaken.
Magic or not?
(A Voyager/HBJ book)
Reprint of the ed. published by Harcourt, Brace
& World, New York.
SUMMARY: An old well that might be magic affords an
exciting summer for the twins, James and Laura, and
helps them to right an ancient wrong.
[I. Magic–Fiction] I. Bodecker, N. M.
II. Title.
[PZ7.E115Maj 1979]   [Fic]   78-71152
ISBN 0-15-655121-7

B C D E F G H I J

For Kip and Jeremy Gould

CONTENTS

MAGIC OR NOT?

1. The Wishing Well

Laura sat looking out of the window, watching houses and barns and woods wheel slowly by, as the tiny train chugged uphill.

If you had seen her sitting there, with her square frame and her square forehead and her square-cut thick dark hair, you would have thought she looked like a solid, dependable girl, and you would have been right, but there was more to Laura than that. Behind the square forehead her thoughts were adventurous. Now she bounced on the seat impatiently. When would they get there?

Her brother James came down the aisle and squeezed in next to her. "Seventeen minutes exactly," he said, looking at his watch and answering her unspoken question. James always knew things exactly. If he didn't know, he found out. Right now he had been in conference with the conductor.

"Seventeen minutes more, and a whole new life will unfold!" gloated Laura. "Oh, James, isn't it going to be wonderful?"

"Wait and see," said James. He was never one to commit himself.

"Oh, James," said Laura again, in tones of disgust. Neither she nor anyone else had ever called James "Jimmy," or even "Jim," but it wasn't for the reasons you might think. He wasn't stodgy or prissy or no fun; James was a leader. With his broad shoulders and his steady blue eyes and his firm jaw he looked serious and practical and he was, but that wasn't all there was to it. Behind the blue eyes his thoughts were deep.

"I found out all about it," he went on. "There're five stops before we get there. The trains aren't always dinky little one-car ones like this; in rush hours there're two cars and sometimes three. They leave every hour on the hour. Here. Have a timetable."

Laura put the timetable in her pocket and stored the information away in her mind. She and James both liked useful facts; you could never tell when they might come in handy, though why, once they were really settled in the country, they would ever want to take a train away from it, Laura couldn't imagine. To live in the country had been her heart's desire ever since she could remember, and now they were actually moving there. Today was moving day. In seventeen, no, fifteen, minutes now, they would *be* there. Laura bounced in her seat again.

"Cemetery!" cried the conductor, and the one car that called itself a train ground to a halt. Laura wondered if a town could really be called Cemetery and what it felt like to live there. She caught James's eye and giggled.

"Think how the people's friends must feel, addressing Christmas cards to them there!" said James, just as if she had spoken aloud. He and Laura could often read each other's minds. Maybe it was because they were twins, though not identical.

"It's even better than looking alike," Laura often said. "We've got identical minds."

"Not exactly," James would remind her. "Who didn't get A in Arithmetic?"

"Oh, that!" Laura would toss her head. "Who would want to?"

But today her mind and James's were like two hearts that beat as one, and she knew he was every bit as excited as she was, though he didn't let on. It was exciting to be on the train by themselves, and it was exciting

to be moving (though they had done that every Octo-
ber first, anyway, back in the city), but to be moving to
the country was the excitement beside which all
others paled.

The way they were moving was interesting in itself.
First the big van had left early that morning with all
the furniture, then the brand-new secondhand car with
Mother and Father and Deborah who was the baby in
the front seat, and all the suitcases piled in back. There
were lots of suitcases, and that was why James and
Laura had to come on the train.

"And which of us will get there first," Father had
said, "is in the lap of providence. You've got your key."

Standing on the sidewalk in front of the apartment
house and waving after the disappearing car, Laura had
felt suddenly very empty and deserted, but only for a
moment.

"Don't look back," James had counseled wisely,
hailing a taxi in an offhand and independent manner.
And then came Grand Central Station and crowds, and
the fast express train, and changing at Stamford, which
was in Connecticut but didn't look like country at all,
and now here they were on the last lap of the journey
that was to bring them to their first sight of the red
house.

They knew it was red and they knew it was old, but
that was all they knew.

All Laura's friends thought she was perfectly fool-hardy to be moving off to the country without looking at the house first, but Laura had wanted it that way.

After their first weekend of scouring the countryside with their parents, she and James had decided that house-hunting was not for them. "The trouble is," said Laura, "we fall in love with each new place, and then there's always something wrong with it, and we don't take it, and we're left wondering what would have happened if we *had!* We can't go round all our lives being homesick for a lot of houses we've never lived in! It's too much to expect." And James had agreed.

"Remember the wonderful big yellow house with the lake?" said Laura to James now, as they rode along.

"It had termites," said James.

"And the one that used to be a barn, with the three-story living room?"

"The porch sagged," said James, "and there was a dead fox in the auxiliary well."

"Do you suppose this one'll be even half as good?"

"It's older. It was built way back before the Revolution. George Washington had his Connecticut head-quarters there," James reminded her.

"It must be full of history," Laura agreed.

"Maybe it's haunted," said James hopefully.

"Or magic. Like Seekings House, where Kay Harker lived," said Laura, looking down at her train book, which was *The Midnight Folk*, that wonderful story by Mr. John Masefield. She was rereading it for the third time.

"No." James shook his head regretfully. "I guess that would be too much to expect. You never hear about magic happening to anybody any more. I guess it's had its day."

"Are you *sure?*" said a voice.

James and Laura looked up, startled.

A face was regarding them over the back of the seat just ahead. It was a girl's face, thin and sunburned, with high cheekbones and wide-set grey eyes. Long, straight fair hair hung down on each side of the face, giving it an old-fashioned appearance.

"What did you say?" stammered Laura.

"I said what makes you so sure?" said the girl the face belonged to. "Just 'cause magic never happened to *you,* it doesn't mean it isn't lurking around still, waiting to turn up when you least expect it!"

"What do *you* know about it?" said James, with surprising rudeness, Laura thought.

"A lot," said the girl. "I ought to. My grandmother's a witch."

"Humph!" said James, who seemed to have taken a dislike to the strange girl.

"Wait and see, that's all!" said the girl. "Drop a wish in the wishing well, and wait and see!" And she clambered down from the seat she'd been kneeling on and went loping long-leggedly past them toward the end of the car.

Before they could make up their minds to follow, the conductor was calling, "Last stop! All out!" and the aisle was clogged with homing travellers. By the time James and Laura could catch up their goods and chattels and the game of Scrabble they'd bought to while away the flagging hours, the strange girl had vanished.

But from the platform Laura caught sight of her again, all the way across the station yard. She was jumping into a big high-shouldered car that looked ancient enough to be obsolete at *least*. Laura couldn't see the person driving the car very well, but she got an impression of a gaunt, weather-beaten face and flyaway grey hair.

"Look!" she cried, squeezing James's arm and pointing. "That must be her grandmother. She *does* look like a witch!"

James paid her no heed. He was striding along with the stubborn look of practical common sense on his face that he always wore when he didn't want to be bothered with some girlish foolishness; so Laura held her peace.

But in the taxicab she brought up the subject again. "She seemed to know all about what house we're going to," she said. "How do you suppose she knew there's a wishing well?"

"Maybe there isn't," said James. "She was prob'ly

just making the whole thing up. Or if she wasn't, well, she heard us say all that about George Washington, didn't she? The house must be pretty famous if he had his headquarters there."

"I don't know," said Laura. "From what I've heard, he seems to have slept in a lot of houses. I guess he was pretty sociable."

They had left the little town behind now, and there were woods and fields, with a house or two every so often. The taxicab turned a corner and James read the sign at one side. "Silvermine Road!" he said. "That's where we're going."

All thought of the strange girl was forgotten as he and Laura peered ahead, looking for red houses.

And at last they saw one, and it turned out to be the right one, and the taxicab stopped at the gate. The house was long and low and there was a white picket fence with hollyhocks.

"And look!" cried Laura excitedly. "See the wishing well!"

"I see a well," said James cautiously, paying the cab driver.

There was no sign of the moving van or the family car; so James got out his key and marched purposefully up the flagged path, while Laura lingered, looking at the flowers that grew all around the house and wondering what the uncommon ones were. She had never had a garden.

But she caught up with James by the time he got the key to turn in the stiff lock, and they pushed forward together over the threshold into cool darkness.

To pull up the blinds was the work of but a moment, and then all was discovery and conquest.

"Dibs on this room!" said James, running up the steep stairway and finding a long, low, sloping-roofed, dormered bedroom that had been made by throwing two smaller rooms together. Luckily there was another room just like it right next door that could be Laura's; so *that* was all right.

And downstairs the living room had an immense fireplace that was big enough to stand up in (because James tried), with an old-fashioned crane and a Dutch oven.

"And probably a secret room somewhere to hide from the Tories in!" said Laura. But though they pushed and pulled at the woodwork, no panel slid aside and no door popped open; so they went outdoors again.

James gave the well (wishing or otherwise) a wide berth and a contemptuous look and strode on to the back of the house, and Laura followed. The back yard stretched itself grassily out, with plenty of room for croquet and badminton both, *besides* a long flower border at each side and a rock garden at the far end that merged into a stony wood that seemed to go on forever.

" 'This is the forest primeval, the murmuring pines and the hemlocks,' " said Laura.

"Only it's birch and maple mostly," said James, who,

though a city boy, had been a Boy Scout and was knowledgeable about such things. "There're three acres of land altogether. I remember, from when Father signed the deed for the house."

"Who," said Laura, "could ask for anything more?"

Part of James and Laura wanted to stay and explore the wood right now and see what wild flowers grew there (Laura) and what was the best place for camping out (James). But there was another part of them that couldn't settle down to doing any one thing for very long today, which is a feeling you may have noticed yourself on your first day in a new place.

Now James said he thought he'd walk up the road and meet Father and Mother and Deborah, and Laura said it was too hot for walking and she'd rather go back inside and explore some more and make plans and reconnoiter, so they separated.

Inside the house Laura felt wonderfully in charge and monarch of all she surveyed. It was like playing house when she was little, only real. First she went upstairs to her bedroom and arranged all the furniture in her mind's eye. Then she went down to the living room and pretended it was a winter evening and they were all sitting round the fire with a north wind howling outside. Then she went into the dining room to see what the view would be every morning from the breakfast table. After that she felt like sitting down, only there weren't any chairs; so she went and perched on the front-hall staircase. But the stairs weren't very comfortable, and after a bit she began to realize that waiting alone in an unfurnished house can have its spooky side, with nothing happening but empty listening silence and motes of dust filtering through the sunlight and collecting on the floor.

She went outside again and looked up and down the road. There was no sign of James. Still, it was a winding road; probably he'd just turned round a corner. Laura decided to stroll as far as the nearest bend and look for him. But first she crossed the road to the woodsy, brambly, thorny thicket just opposite to take another look at the house and get used to the fact that it was home now. And it was then that her glance fell on the well, and she remembered the strange girl on the train again.

She went back across the road and into her own yard. The well *looked* the way a wishing well ought to look, with its small, gabled, vine-clad roof built over the wellhead and a rope hanging down inside. Laura peered over the edge and thought she saw the bucket, halfway down.

"Why not?" she said aloud, to air and grass and roses and a catbird in an elderbush.

She was the kind of girl who always had a pencil in her pocket, and to find a scrap of old shelf-paper in the kitchen was the work of a moment. But deciding what to wish wasn't so easy.

Being a well-brought-up girl, Laura had read plenty of fairy tales, and had always been loud in her scorn of the people in them who wasted their wishes on black puddings and wanting to be beautiful as the day or have pockets lined with gold. She had always been sure she could manage better than *that*, when her time came. Yet now that it *had* come, her mind was a blank.

After all, she reasoned with herself, it didn't have to be something big and important to start out with. Any common everyday wish would do for a sample, to test the well and see if it had the right stuff in it. Then if it did, she could tell James and they'd plan everything out, and the really important magic of the summer could begin.

Laura had got this far in her thoughts when she heard a shout and a rattle. She looked up. A car was just coming round the bend. Laura could tell it was *their* car by the bicycles strapped to the roof. And besides, James was riding on the running board (it was an old enough car to *have* running boards, not one of your modern streamlined finny monsters where all attempts to find toehold are a vain mockery). And Deborah was hanging out a window and calling something unintelligible in her hoarse bass voice that was always such a shock to strangers, coming from her pretty baby face.

Laura thought quickly. Only a second more and they would be there. And if James arrived on the scene and saw how childish she was being, she would never live it down. And Deborah would want to know all about it and butt in.

Without more ado, she scribbled the first six words that came into her head. The words were, "I wish I had a kitten." It was a dull wish, but her own. And if there *were* magic, and it chose to be difficult and turn against her, the way magic so often did in books, Laura didn't see how a wish like that could do any harm. A kitten would always come in handy. She crumpled the paper into a ball, tossed it down the well, and ran to open the gate.

And then Moving Day began in earnest.

First there were all the heavy suitcases to lug into the house and put in the right rooms. And before James and Laura were half finished with that, the moving van arrived, and all was loud tramping and heavy breathing and dull thuds and keeping Deborah out from under the movingmen's feet.

And when the men finally left, there were the suitcases to unpack and clothes to be put away in bureau drawers, and the china barrels to unload and all the dishes to be washed and stacked on shelves, and after that most of the furniture had to be moved from the places where they'd told the moving men to put it to the other places where on second thought they all agreed it looked lots better.

It was late in the afternoon when the family assembled dustily in the living room.

"The things from the apartment look kind of skimpy in all this space, don't they?" said James.

"Never mind. We'll find wonderful things here. There'll be auctions," said their mother, the gleam of the antique-hunter in her eye.

"Auctions!" James and Laura savored the word, remembering sundry movies in which people went to auctions and bought old chests that contained maps of buried treasure in secret drawers.

"What's an auction?" said Deborah.

"Generally," said their father, collapsing on the sofa and flicking a curlicue of china-packing newspaper from his right eyebrow, "it is a snare and a delusion. Never have I been so weary. I thought tonight we'd all go out to dinner. Now I doubt if I can face it."

Their mother looked round at their tired faces. "Baths for everybody," she announced, "and pajamas and early bed. There's canned soup in the carton with the pots and pans."

"You think of everything," said their father admiringly.

The canned soup was tomato and pea mixed, which is delicious. It was consumed in silence, save for the crunching of saltines. And then everyone staggered upstairs.

Laura was brushing her hair dreamily before her dressing-table mirror when she heard the hoofbeats. She ran to the window.

It was night, but the moon had risen. In the moonlight a black horse galloped along the edge of the road past the house (keeping off the pavement, which is bad for horses' hoofs). And riding the horse, her fair hair streaming on the wind, was a girl. It was the girl from the train.

"She *is* magic!" gasped Laura. "Something's going to happen!"

She would have run for the wishing well, but the horse and the girl were gone now. The hoofbeats died away in the distance. Laura decided she'd sit down on the bed for a minute first. Then she decided she'd lie back on the pillow, just for a second.

How long after that it was that she heard the sound, Laura never knew. It was a creaking sound, just the kind of noise that magic might make if it were winding the bucket up from its watery depths to get at the wish. But would magic do that? Wouldn't it sooner dive down the well and grant the wish from there? Or even more likely, wouldn't it live at the bottom and catch the wishes as they came down?

She must run to the window again and see what was happening. Any second now she *would*. But sleep was all around her, like a downy, feathery, pillowy cloud. She sank into it.

The next thing she knew, it was morning.

2. The Witch's Garden

It will hardly be believed that Laura didn't leap from her bed with her first waking thought and rush to the wishing well to see if the noise in the night had been magic and, if so, what it had accomplished. But she didn't.

Waking up for the first time in a new place has a magic of its own that can drive all other thoughts out of your head, and it was that way with Laura.

The first thing she heard when she woke up was a lawn mower and the first thing she thought was, "James!"

It was James's habit always to wake up early and get any dull tasks out of the way before settling down to the day's round of pleasure. And Mother had said last night that "that lawn" was a disgrace and positively had to be mowed this morning. And Father had said that there was an old rusty hand-wheeled mower in the shed that "would do" till he got another.

Laura jumped out of bed. Even lawn-mowing has its charms when you've lived in a city apartment all your life and never had a lawn to mow. And besides, there is something about the sound of other people's labor on a sunny July morning that stirs the belated slugabed.

Laura hurried through breakfast and dishes and ran out the back door, slamming the screen behind her. Then she stopped short.

Sitting on a rock watching James work was a strange boy. The boy had curly yellow hair and a beagle dog. He was sucking a popsickle, grape from the color. He and James were not communicating, but James's back as he pushed the mower along had a self-conscious look, as if he were all too aware of his audience.

"Boys!" thought Laura. "Honestly! They'd probably just stay like that all day and never say a word to each other if somebody sensible didn't come along!"

She walked up to the strange boy. "My name's Laura," she said. "What's yours?"

"Kip," said the boy.

"Short for Christopher?" said Laura.

"That's right," said the boy.

James stopped mowing and came nearer, but warily, as if the boy might bite.

"What's your dog's name?" said Laura.

"Alice," said the boy.

"Why?" said Laura. As soon as she'd said it, she knew the answer. "Because she goes down rabbit holes?"

"That's right," said the boy.

Suddenly they all three grinned and relaxed, and after that it was as though they'd known each other all along.

"We just moved here," confided Laura, "from New York."

"I know," said the boy. "We live up the road. I saw the moving van. My Pop works in New York. He's in advertising."

"This is a lousy lawn mower," said James.

"I could see that," said the boy. "I was thinking. Why don't you borrow ours?"

"Power?"

"Sure."

"The kind you sit in and drive?"

"That's right."

"Lead me to it."

"Honestly!" said Laura to herself, as she followed them around the house. "Practically arms-around-the-neck friends now, and he could still be pushing that rusty old thing if I hadn't broken the ice! Honestly, *boys!* Deliver *me!*"

They walked up the road, the dog Alice trotting on before, looking back over her shoulder every few steps and smiling to see that they were still there. Just around the first bend they passed an old rutted driveway James didn't remember noticing before. It wound up over a hill to disappear in dark woods. "Who lives there?" he wondered.

"Lydia Green," said Kip. "She's crazy."

"Crazy?" said James.

"Well, not crazy exactly. Kind of wild," said Kip. "She lives with her grandmother. She can't do a thing with her."

"Who can't do a thing with which?" said James.

"Neither one," said Kip.

They both giggled. "Like a couple of fools," sniffed Laura to herself. Then she had a sudden thought. "This Lydia. Does she have long hair? Does she ride a black horse?"

"Night and day," said Kip. "My mother says it's a scandal."

"I think we met her on the train," said Laura. "I think I saw her again last night. Her grandmother's a witch, she said."

"Nah," said Kip. "Just an artist. She's kind of eccentric, though. They both are."

"Oh," said Laura.

She would have gone on, to tell about the wishing well and the wish she'd made, but the boys were deep in talk about power mowers again. And besides, they would laugh at her. And besides, they were turning into Kip's driveway now.

Kip's house was old, but not so old as theirs, and painted light yellow with white shutters. His mother seemed to be an understanding type, and the power mower was secured without hostilities.

Back at the red house, James and Laura took turns using it. Neither of them had ever even seen a power mower close up before, and learning how to run it was exciting, so exciting that Laura again forgot all about the girl on the train. The whole back yard and most of the side were finished before her first fine careless rapture flagged.

"I'll run it awhile now, if you're both tired," volunteered Kip, and he headed the mower toward the front of the house.

"He's nice, isn't he?" said Laura to James.

"He's a good kid," said James.

"Do you suppose he'll be our best friend?" said Laura. "Do you suppose we'll go on wonderful, exciting adventures together?"

"Holy gee!" said James. "What good does it do, wondering about things like that? Wait and see." He snorted. "Honestly. Girls!"

"Hey," called Kip, from the front yard. "Hey, this is a dangerous place to leave kittens."

"What?" said James.

"*What?*" said Laura, in a different tone. She caught her breath and her eyes shone.

They both ran round the house to where Kip stood by the well. He had climbed down from the mower and was bending over something on the edge of the stone wellhead.

James and Laura crowded close. What he was looking at was a basket with a lid, and from under the lid came a mewing sound.

"Let me," said Laura. She lifted the lid. Inside the basket was a squirming piebald bundle that untangled itself and turned into two kittens, a black one and a white.

"Night and Day," said Kip.

"Shadow and Substance," said James.

"No such thing," said Laura. "It's Blackmalkin and Whitemalkin. They're magic." And then and there she told the other two all about the wishing well and her wish and the night ride of the girl Lydia and the creaking sound she'd heard afterwards.

"Double Magic," said Kip. "You only wished for one. That's better than Half by a long shot."

"Oh, have you read that, too?" said Laura, for the book called *Half Magic* was one of her favorites.

"Sure," said Kip. "I guess just about everyone has."

"I don't know," said James. "Prob'ly they're not magic at all. Prob'ly it's all a hoax. Prob'ly that girl Lydia did it."

Laura was turning the handle that wound up the rope that brought up the bucket. "She couldn't have," she said, as it came into view. "There's my wish, all crumpled up, just the way I threw it in."

"It made a creaking sound when you wound it," said James. "That's what you heard last night. Prob'ly that Lydia crumpled the wish up and let it down again after she'd read it."

"It would be just like her," said Kip. "She's kind of crafty."

"I don't believe it," said Laura. "I'm going to go over there right now and ask her." And she marched out of the gate and up the road, slightly impeded by the kittens that were crawling up her front and wreathing themselves around her neck.

"Here, let me carry one," said Kip, catching up with her.

"You can take Whitemalkin," said Laura. "Blackmalkin's mine."

James appeared on Laura's other side. He was carrying the empty basket. "Important evidence," he said, swinging it round his head. "Exhibit A!"

They rounded the bend in the road and turned into the overgrown driveway that said "Green" on an old faded sign half-hidden by a tangle of poison ivy.

"What'll you wish for next if the magic's real?" said Kip. "Do you suppose you get three wishes each? Do you suppose *I* get to wish, too? Or would it be just for the actual owners, do you suppose?"

"If it's only three wishes," said James to Laura, "you've wasted one already. Kittens!"

"They're *not* a waste!" said Laura indignantly, stroking Blackmalkin.

"Purr," said Blackmalkin.

"Ickle poo," said Laura, ruffling the fur under its chin.

"Ugh!" said James, turning away from the sickening sight.

The dog Alice trotted before them. She had welcomed the arrival of the kittens philosophically, as she did all the strange happenings of the wonderful human world. But now suddenly she stopped in her tracks. Her hackles, if that was the right word, rose. She whined and muttered in her throat. It was eerie.

The three children stopped, too, and looked where Alice was looking.

In the woodsy shadows of the drive ahead, a figure was stumping along. At first it seemed bent out of all human form, but as it came nearer, they saw that it was an old woman with flyaway grey hair. The reason she looked so lopsided was that she was carrying an easel and an immense blank canvas and an oversize paintbox. All three things kept slipping and had to be hoisted.

"It's the grandmother," hissed Laura to James. "It's the old witch!"

"Shush," hissed James to Laura. "Good morning, ma'am," he said aloud, as the figure came within earshot. Alice got behind Kip and pretended to be invisible.

Old Mrs. Green did not appear to have heard James. She was glaring at the woods by the side of the drive. "Maple trees, maple trees," she was muttering, "that's all there is to paint around here!" Then she seemed to notice the three children for the first time and regarded them with a piercing gaze. "If you're giving away cats," she said, "we don't want any. I can't abide 'em."

Laura was outraged. "We're *not* giving them away," she said. "I wouldn't give them away for *anything*. And they're not cats, they're kittens."

"*That* won't last," said old Mrs. Green. "That's the tragedy of it."

"Can I help you carry those things, ma'am?" asked Kip politely.

Old Mrs. Green let the piercing gaze dwell on him for a long time. "Young man," she said at last, "I've been toting this truck around since before you were born. I plan to go on doing it for a few years still!" She started past them. Then she seemed to relent and turned. "If you're looking for Lydia," she said, "she's in the barn with that fool horse. Pesky thing. *I* say it's got the evil eye!" And she went stumping on down the driveway. "Maple trees, maple trees, I swear I'll move to Maine!" the three children heard her muttering. Then she was gone.

Laura and James and Kip looked at each other and giggled. But the giggle was halfhearted. Old Mrs. Green was funny, but there was more to her than that. Witch or not, she was a character. Meeting a character ought to make a promising start to any morning, and yet the feet of the three children lagged as they went on up the driveway. Alice hung behind and whimpered.

Around the next bend they came in sight of the house. It was a big house, built in the hideous beetle-browed style of 1905. Leggy, unclipped shrubs masked its windows, and overgrown vines clung to the eaves and had their way with the shingles.

"It must be dark as pitch inside," said Laura.

To one side of the house was a big sagging barn, and coming from its doorway now was the girl Lydia. She wore riding breeches, an old patched flannel shirt, and a frown that deepened as she saw James and Laura and Kip.

"Oh," she said.

"Well?" said James.

"What do you want?" said the girl.

"As if you didn't know," said James.

Kip was more diplomatic. "We wanted to have a talk," he said.

For some reason this seemed to make the strange girl

Lydia even crosser. "Go away," she told him, in what was almost a snarl. She turned her back on him and spoke to Laura and James. "I suppose you've heard all about me by now. Nobody in this town has any use for me and I haven't any use for *them*."

Something about the way she said it made Laura want to be nicer. She didn't care if the boys believed or not. "It worked!" she said, smiling at the girl and holding up Blackmalkin.

Lydia regarded her coldly. "What worked?"

"The magic!" said Laura. "The wishing well, just the way you said! I wished for a kitten and got two!"

"Just as if you didn't know *that!*" said James.

"I don't know what you mean," said Lydia.

Laura refused to be dampened. "This one's Blackmalkin," she said, holding the black kitten up, "and the other one's Whitemalkin."

"Like *The Midnight Folk*," said Lydia, with her first approach to being human.

"Oh, have you read that, too?" Laura beamed, and even James relaxed a little.

"Dozens of times," said Lydia.

"I never heard of it," said Kip.

"You wouldn't," said Lydia, without looking at him.

Laura felt discouraged again. "The trouble is," she said, "they think you rode over on your horse in the night and read the wish and left the kittens there to fool us."

"Do they?" said Lydia. "What do *you* think?"

"I thought so, too, for a while," admitted Laura. Then she made up her mind. "Now I don't any more." She touched the kitten's fur. "I know *I* couldn't give Blackmalkin away to *anyone!* So how could *you?*"

Lydia regarded the black kitten with rather a strange expression. "Yes," she said. "Yes, there *is* that." Then she seemed to shrug the whole problem away. "Well," she said, "so now you know. You've got magic. Have fun with it." And she started for the house.

"Wait!" cried Laura.

Lydia turned and looked at her. Laura didn't know how to say what she wanted to say. "Couldn't we share it?"

"How do you mean?"

"Couldn't we sort of have our wishes together? All four of us? It'd be more fun."

Lydia looked as though she couldn't believe her ears. But James was still suspicious.

"Or even better," he said, "couldn't you show us some of your magic right here, without any old well?"

The friendliness went out of Lydia's eyes. "I don't know what you mean," she said again.

"You have lots of it, lying around," said James. "You said your grandmother's a witch."

"Did I say that?" Lydia looked shamefaced, then defiant. "Well, she is, sometimes."

"Show us some," said James stubbornly. Laura could

have hit him. Even the good-natured Kip fidgeted uncomfortably.

Lydia looked at the ground. Then she looked up. "All right," she said grimly. "Follow me."

She started past the house, not looking back to see whether they were following or not. Of course they were.

Beyond the house was an old tumble-down stone wall with a gate in it. Lydia opened the gate and went through it and down some steps, with the others trailing after.

"There," she said. "Doesn't that look like a witch's garden?"

It did.

None of the three children knew much about flowers, and only Laura cared about them much, but all of them had seen enough gardens to realize that mostly they were planted three or six or a dozen of a kind, in ordered rows or artistic drifts. Here there were no two plants alike and they grew every which way, big plants in front of small ones, vines clambering over bushes. It was as though nobody cared where or how they grew, so long as they grew. Parts of the garden were weeded, but most of it wasn't. Some of the plants were strange looking, almost evil.

"That's a pitcher plant. It eats flies," said Lydia, pointing. "That's a Venus's-flytrap. So does it."

"That's not magic. That's nature," said James the ex-Boy Scout, unconvinced. "You'll have to do better than that."

"All right," said Lydia. Her jaw was set and her expression was dangerous. "All right, I will!"

"What's *that?*" said Kip, wanting to change the subject. He pointed to a sprawly, branchy, trailing plant with notched leaves and cup-shaped purplish-red flowers.

"That," said Lydia, her eyes taking on a dreamy, other-worldly look, "is crawling rabbitbane. It's one of the most powerful magic plants there is. It's been used by witches from time immemorial."

"What does it *do?*" said James, inexorable.

"It kills rabbits, from the name," said Kip.

"That's right," said Lydia. "It does. It'd kill *you*, too, if you ate it. It's deadly poison. But if you *burnt* it, now . . ." She broke off.

"Now what?" said James. "What if we did?"

"Well," said Lydia slowly, "there's no telling what might happen. It does all kinds of things. It makes unseen things appear and seen things disappear. It transforms people so they're unrecognizable, overnight. And if the right person burns it at the right time and breathes the smoke, it can bring . . ." She stopped again.

"What? What can it bring?" said James.

"A visitor from another world," said Lydia.

"What kind of visitor? A dear little fairy?" scoffed James.

"A genie?" said Laura.

"A Martian?" said Kip.

Lydia stared at them solemnly. "I don't know. Nobody knows. It's not in the magic books."

There was a pause.

"O.K.," said James. "What are we waiting for? Let's be burning."

There were seven flowers on the plant and all were gathered in a second. But burning them didn't prove too easy. The petals shriveled and turned black at the edges and several fingers were scorched, but there was no smoke to speak of (or to breathe).

Then James and Kip made a fire of sticks and paper, and the charred remains of the crawling rabbitbane were cast upon it. The blossoms flared up for a second and were gone, but not before four noses bent over the fire and sniffed. James watched to see if Lydia sniffed, too, and she did. Then four throats coughed. There was smoke all right, but it smelled more like stick-and-paper smoke than anything else.

"Is that all?" said Kip, as careful James stamped out the smoldering ashes.

"What did you expect, fireworks?" said Lydia nastily.

"I thought it'd be different somehow," said Laura.

"I thought magic smoke would smell sort of special. Like in that poem. You know. 'Whiffs of gramarye!'"

Lydia's face lighted up. "Do you know that, too? We seem to have read all the same things!"

"Yes, we do, don't we?" said Laura, beaming at her.

James broke in on this literary discussion. "Well?" he said. "When does it get going? When do the little fairies start turning up?"

The light went out of Lydia's face and it looked closed and hard. "I haven't the slightest idea," she said. "Probably never. Probably we weren't the right people at the right time. Or probably it's all a hoax and I made the whole thing up!"

"Probably," agreed James, grinning at her challengingly.

Laura was alarmed. "No!" She glared at James. "That's silly. It wouldn't happen right *away!* More like tomorrow morning, wouldn't you say?" She turned to Lydia.

"I don't know anything about it," said Lydia stonily. "I have to go feed my horse." And she stalked away.

There was something about the thin, hunched look of her back and shoulders as she rounded the corner of the house that Laura couldn't bear. She ran after her. Then when she caught up with her, she couldn't think of anything to say. She walked along at her side in silence.

"Laura and Lydia," she said finally. "We sound like sisters in a book."

"We don't look it," muttered Lydia.

Laura tried again. "Are you crazy about horseback-riding? Does it sort of rule your whole life?" For she had met girls in real life and in books of whom this was true.

Lydia shrugged. "It's a means to an end."

They were nearing the barn now, and a whinny sounded from inside. Laura hung back. "I'm scared of horses," she confessed.

Lydia looked at her. Suddenly she grinned. "So am I."

"But you ride all the time!" said Laura. "Night and day, Kip said!"

"I know," said Lydia. "That's why." And she started away.

Laura called after her, stammering slightly, not sure how her words would be received. "Could you. . . . could you come over to our house tomorrow morning? I'd. . . . we'd like you to."

Lydia turned in the doorway. She wasn't smiling. She looked as if she were going to say no. But she didn't. "All right," she said. Then she was gone.

Laura ran and overtook the boys just as they were turning from the driveway into the road. She saw no sign of old Mrs. Green. Alice the dog was biffing far ahead of them down the road, as though glad to get away from the witch's house.

"I don't care what anyone says," said Laura, as soon as she got her breath back. "I like her!"

"So do I," said Kip, rather as though he were surprised to hear himself saying it.

They both looked at James.

"All right, so do I," he admitted sheepishly. "If only she didn't have such a chip on her shoulder all the time."

"She's like that in school, too," said Kip. "That's why nobody gets along with her."

"I think . . ." said Laura, stammering slightly the way she always did when she was very serious, "I think she makes things hard for herself. I wonder why."

There was a pause. "Anyway," said Kip, "there's one thing you can't deny. She's interesting."

And all agreed.

And then they all went back to the red house and had sandwiches and did the most un-magic things they could think of all afternoon.

It was nearly dinnertime when Kip went home, but he found his mother still out working in the garden. Kip's mother was like that. She belonged to the Garden Club.

Kip went and hung over her, wanting to know when dinner would be ready and what was for dessert, and making distracting desultory conversation and tracing patterns with his bare toes in the loose gritty black earth of the rock garden until his mother told him to stop.

He stopped, but not for that reason. He was staring at a plant that sprawled over a big rock. It was a branchy, trailing plant with notched leaves and cup-shaped purplish-red flowers.

"I didn't know we had crawling rabbitbane, too," he said.

"What?" said his mother.

"That," said Kip, pointing.

"That," said his mother, "is *Callirrhoë involucrata.*"

"Are you sure? What's its common name?"

"Poppy mallow."

Kip had a sinking feeling. Still, his mother could be wrong. The Garden Club didn't know *everything*. "*I* heard," he said, "that it's called crawling rabbitbane. I heard it's a powerful magic herb. I heard it's been used by witches from time immemorial."

"Humph!" said his mother. "It's a western wild flower. I don't think it's been in cultivation more than fifty years or so. The only magic trick it does that *I* know anything about is sow itself all over the place!" Her thumb and forefinger annihilated half a dozen unwanted seedlings. "There. Now come in the house and wash your hands." And she went inside.

But Kip didn't follow her. He sat down on a garden chair and started thinking hard.

3. The Silver Mine

When Laura came bounding out of the house next morning with James following more sedately at her heels, Kip was already there, sitting on a rock eating a popsickle, orange this time.

"Hello. You must have got up early," said Laura.

"That's right. I guess I did." Kip spoke through a yawn. "No particular reason. I just thought I would. It was such a nice morning and all."

"Oh, is that why?" said James. "I thought maybe it was because you believed all that yesterday. I thought maybe you couldn't wait to meet the dear little fairy."

"James!" said Laura. "Don't you start talking like that when *she* comes."

"Do you suppose she *will?*" said Kip.

"Of course she will," said Laura stoutly.

"I'm not counting on it," said James. "I don't know if she'll have the face."

"Stop it," said Laura. "If you're so sure there isn't any magic, what are you doing here? Why waste your time? Go do something useful. Chop wood or go fishing."

"Oh, I'm open to conviction," said James cheerfully. "That reminds me, though. I'll be back in a second." And he went loping toward the back yard.

Kip finished his popsickle and stuck the stick into the ground. "Surprise for James," he said. "Here she comes now."

Laura looked. Lydia was coming toward them down the road, walking slowly, not riding the black horse this time. ("And that's a good sign," thought Laura to herself. "It shows she doesn't think she has to prove anything to us.")

"Hello," she called.

"Hello," said Lydia, coming up to them.

"Hello," said Kip.

There was a silence. Nobody could think what to say next.

James came round the corner of the house, talking to himself. "That's funny," he was saying.

"What is?" called Kip.

"That old lawn mower I was using. I forgot to put it away yesterday. Now it's not in the shed or anywhere."

"That's funny," echoed Kip. "Who would want to steal a rusty old thing like that?"

James came toward them, walking with his head down the way he always did when he was concentrating. He was concentrating so hard he almost ran into a young maple sapling that stood in the middle of the lawn. He stopped short just in time and stood looking at it.

"That wasn't here yesterday," he said.

"Don't be silly; of course it was," said Laura.

"No." James was a very observant kind of boy. "I made a mental map of the whole front yard. That tree wasn't there."

"It must have been. Trees don't move by themselves!" said Laura. Then she caught her breath. "The magic! Don't you remember? It makes unseen things appear and seen things disappear! It's *working!*"

"It is?" Lydia sounded surprised, almost alarmed.

"Sure. Didn't you think it would?" said Kip, giving her rather a peculiar look, Laura thought.

James went up to Lydia and held out his hand. "I apologize," he said.

Lydia looked at his hand as if she didn't want to take it. Then she made a grab for it and dropped it again quickly. "That's all right," she muttered, looking away.

"I don't get the point, though," said James, scratching his head. "Why would the magic go to all that effort just to take away an old lawnmower and give us an old maple tree? We've *got* enough maple trees!"

" 'Maple trees, maple trees, that's all there is around here!' " quoted Kip, giggling. "It's a better maple tree than the lawn mower was a lawn mower, anyway," he pointed out.

"No, don't you see?" said Laura excitedly. "This isn't the real magic. It's just showing us it's here. So we'll be prepared. The real wonderful part'll come later!"

"What was it you said would happen next?" said James to Lydia.

"I don't remember," said Lydia, looking at the ground.

"You *don't?* I'll never forget!" said Laura. "It makes unseen things appear and seen things disappear," she repeated in thrilling tones. "It transforms people so they're unrecognizable, overnight. And if the right person burns it at the right time . . ." She broke off, staring across the lawn.

Deborah was trotting toward them from the woods to one side. Deborah was the kind of four-year-old girl who gets up at the crack of dawn and plays happily by herself for hours, and nobody worries much about where she is or what she's doing. Now as she came nearer, Laura uttered a cry.

"Your hair! What have you been doing to yourself?"

Where once had been tight black pigtails was short hair cut straight across in back in the classic style known as mixing-bowl.

"It wasn't me," said Deborah happily. "It was magic. I'm transformed."

"That," said James, "is putting it mildly. Pretty amateurish magic, if you ask me. You're unrecognizable all right. You look terrible."

"*I* like it," said Deborah, trotting past them to begin another of her mysterious solitary games under the apple tree at the far end of the yard.

Kip giggled.

James gave him a sharp look. Suddenly everything seemed to fall into place in his mind. "Uh *huh*," he said grimly. He strode over to the maple sapling and checked. "I thought so. New-dug earth. Magic wouldn't have to do a thing like that." He went back to Kip. "Let's see your hands."

Kip looked as if he didn't know whether to giggle now or not. He held out his hands. They were suspiciously clean, as if he'd just scrubbed them.

Laura was the last to realize what was in James's mind. "Oh," she cried. "Do you mean it isn't true?"

Lydia pushed past her. Her eyes blazed at Kip as if she would like to pummel him. "Do you mean to say," she said, her voice trembling, "that you got up early this morning and hid the lawn mower and spent all that time and work planting that tree and then cut off that little girl's hair just to play a trick on *me?*"

"No. It wasn't that. Honest," said Kip. "I just didn't want the game to stop."

"A *game?*" wailed Laura. "Is that all it was to everybody?"

"I found out that plant wasn't crawling rabbitbane," Kip went on. "I found out there's no such a thing. And I was kind of sorry. I thought maybe I could sort of rescue you. The tree and all that were all I could think of to do. I guess it wasn't very good. But what would you have done if I hadn't? When the time came?"

"I don't know," said Lydia. "I guess I hoped something would turn up. I guess I hoped if I wished hard enough it'd be true."

"You read the wish in the wishing well and left the kittens, didn't you?" said James.

"Of course I did," said Lydia crossly. "I'm sorry now I started the whole thing. I'm going home. Good-by."

"Wait!" Laura turned on James. "You think you're so right always. She didn't do it to be mean. She did it to make friends. *Didn't* you?" She looked at Lydia.

"Ha! As if I'd be that soft!"

"You were. You did."

"All right, I did," said Lydia. She looked away. Her voice was indistinct. "But it didn't work out. I can't make friends. I never can. I don't know how."

"You do, too. We *are* friends. *Aren't* we?" Laura looked at James threateningly.

"Sure. I'm not mad at anybody," said James mildly. "I just like to get the facts straight." He went over to Lydia. "I apologized once before. This time is for real. Now that we all know the worst about each other, we can start over from scratch."

Lydia hesitated, still looking at something in the far distance. Then she relaxed. "All right," she said.

"You must have hated giving up the kittens," said Laura. "You can have Whitemalkin back if you like."

"I'm sorry about Deborah's hair," said Kip. "I thought it'd turn out better. *She* likes it, though," he added, his eyes twinkling.

"I don't know what Mother'll say when she sees it," said Laura. "Still I guess all's well that ends well."

She looked around at the others. All of them were smiling. And then suddenly the brightness went out of the day. Now that she had ironed out the awful crossness and got everybody else's ruffled feelings smoothed, she had time to remember her own disappointment.

"I *am* sorry about the magic, though," she said. "We could have had all this, and that, too!"

Lydia's hand tightened on her arm. "Look!" she said.

Laura looked.

Coming down the road was a strange apparition.

An ancient horse pulled an ancient carriage of the type that is known as a chaise (or in the poem of the same name, a one-hoss shay). Sitting in the carriage was a lady. Whether she was old or young was hard to tell. Her face was lined but very pretty. Her dress with its wide-flowing long skirts was old-fashioned, but its lemon-yellow-and-scarlet color scheme was youthfully bright, not to say gaudy. Her white hair was worn in a towering pompadour topped by an immense straw hat covered with artificial poppies. The top canopy of the chaise was missing (probably age had withered it, thought James), and the lady carried a flowered parasol to shield her complexion from the sun.

"A visitor from another world!" breathed Laura.

"Looks as if," said Kip, staring with round eyes.

The lady chirruped to her horse, and it stopped directly in front of the red house. The lady smiled at them. "Good morning, children," she said.

"Good morning," said James and Kip and Laura.

Lydia stepped forward.

"Did you come because we wished you would?" she said. It sounded bald, put like that, but she had to know.

"Well, now," said the lady, "did I or didn't I? That's a question. Certainly I have not driven down to the valley for some time. I think it is three years now. Or is it two? No, I think it is three. And certainly this morn-

ing *something* seemed to tell me it was time to venture forth and look at the world again. But whether it was your wish, or the fine summer weather, or something else entirely, I would not be prepared to say. But why do you say you wished for me?"

"We were playing a game," said Kip. "Kind of a wishing game."

"We wished for a visitor from another world," said Laura.

"Another world?" For a moment the lady seemed to be looking beyond them, at faraway things. "Yes, it was certainly that. A better world I *don't* say, but different it *was*. And slower. And more gracious, I like to think."

"When was this?" said James, who liked to get at the facts. "And where?"

"Why, right here," said the lady. "All up and down the valley, when I was young. We may have been country people, but we had pleasant times!"

"And you still live right here somewhere?" said James. There was a touch of disappointment in his voice.

"Certainly I do," said the lady. "Pa always said to me, 'Isabella, whatever happens, never sell the old place.' And I never have. I live across the river and up the hill. By the old silver mine."

"A silver mine!" said James and Laura together.

"Gee!" said James. "I didn't know there was one."

"Sure," said Kip. "What did you think the road was named for?"

"Yeah, sure," said James. "I never thought, the way they've got it all one word on the signs. Silvermine."

"Very slipshod," said the lady. "It would never have been allowed in my day."

"Only I thought that old mine was all abandoned and fallen in," said Kip. "I thought it was played out."

The lady tightened her lips. "It has certainly not been abandoned by *me*," she said. "It may not be working at the moment, and certain portions may have collapsed slightly, but I should never describe it as '*played out*.' Though many a child has played *in* it, in his day, if you will forgive the pun," she added.

"Do you *own* it?" said Lydia. "Could *we* play in it?"

"Certainly I own it," said the lady. "Pa always said to me, 'Isabella, whatever happens, hang on to Kingdom Mine. Mark my words, it will come into its own again some day.' And so I truly believe. As to your playing in it, come any time. Come this afternoon for tea. I shall make my silver cake."

"Isn't it dangerous?" said Laura. "Playing in the mine, I mean."

"Tush!" said the lady. "Show me the thing worth doing that *isn't!*"

A stripped-down convertible full of teen-agers whizzed past down the road, taking the bend on two wheels. The old horse shied and rolled its eyes, but the lady spoke to it soothingly and it subsided.

"Humph!" said the lady. "Don't speak to me of *danger! We* knew how to proceed with dignity." She sighed. "I believe I have seen quite enough of the world for this year. Besides, I must be getting home if I'm to make my silver cake. I shall expect you"—and she bowed formally—"at half-past three."

"We'll be there," said Lydia.

The lady turned her horse, using the reins expertly. Her eyes swept over the front garden. "I see you have a wishing well," she said.

"Yes, but it doesn't work. We thought it did, but it doesn't," said Laura.

"Don't be too sure," said the lady. "You never can tell with wells. *Good* day." She chirruped to the horse and it went trotting with surprising agility back the way it had come.

"*Well!*" said Laura, when horse and lady were out of sight.

"Was it magic?" said Lydia.

"How could it be?" said Kip. "She wasn't supernatural or anything. She was just a person."

"That doesn't signify," said Laura. "She's from another world, isn't she? She said so. The magic could have made her come, couldn't it? She *said* something made her."

Everybody looked at James. Already he was the leader.

"Magic or not," said James, "we've got an adventure, and that's what we wanted. A silver mine. Wow!"

It was five minutes to three when James and Kip and Laura and Lydia started out from the red house. No one could bear to wait any longer. There had been some discussion earlier about what clothes they should wear on the adventure. Laura had wanted to dress up, as it was a tea party, but the others had been derisive.

"Play clothes for playing in mines," said James, and Laura had seen the sense in this. But she carried a bouquet of blue larkspurs as a mark of esteem. Alice the dog did not accompany them, having an engagement elsewhere with a rabbit.

"Which way's the river?" said James, as their feet hit the road. "I didn't even know there was one."

"Follow Bonga Bonga the native guide," said Kip, leading the way with that other old settler, Lydia.

The four children followed where the road wandered, going past houses and a riding stable and a general store and an old tavern that was now a tearoom. Beyond the tavern a road led over a bridge.

They stopped on the bridge and looked down. Underneath were rocks mainly, with a thin stream winding among them.

"Call that a river?" said James.

"Wait till spring floods," said Kip. "It's a river."

Three wild ducks flew over, just to prove it.

After the bridge the road divided, the main trafficky part going on ahead, while a narrower way turned to the left and went twistingly uphill. A sign with a pointing arrow was neatly labeled, "To the Kingdom."

"That must be it," said Laura. "She said 'Kingdom Mine.'"

First the road was sort of paved, then it broke down to just a double wheel-track, with grass in between. The grade was steep and there was a general huffing and puffing, particularly from Kip who, while not fat, was pleasingly plump. At last came a level stretch, and at its end a small house, with a mailbox that said "Miss Isabella King" in the same neat lettering as the sign at the corner.

James and Lydia and Kip collapsed breathlessly on the pocket-handkerchief lawn, while Laura stood and considered the house. Everything that took money to do was neglected, but everything that could be done by one pair of hands was spick and span. The paint on the house was peeling, but the walk was freshly swept. The big dooryard elm tree was dying, but the small lawn was neatly mowed and its edges clipped.

Laura had rather thought that Miss Isabella King might be on the porch to greet them, but there was no sign of her. Probably she was getting tea.

James rose from his prone position on the lawn, crossing his long legs and rising straight up the way he always did. "Enough of dalliance," he said. "I breathe again. Let's get with it." He mounted the steps to the porch, and since he was the leader, the others followed.

Miss Isabella King was slow in answering their knock, and when she did appear, she seemed strangely altered from their visitor of that morning. She still wore the yellow-and-scarlet dress, though she had taken off the hat with the poppies. But her white pompadour was disarranged as though she had just been lying down, and her face was pale and her hands fidgeted nervously. ("And it's *my* opinion," said Kip later, "that she had been *crying*.")

"Oh dear," she said. "I do apologize. And Pa always said hospitality is the first duty of a gentlewoman, too! Nowadays I receive so few visitors, you would think I would be ready to greet you, and yet the time had quite slipped my mind! The fact is, I have had some very upsetting news by today's post."

"I'm sorry," said Laura.

"Not that I had forgotten you were coming," said Miss King quickly. "I have my silver cake all baked and frosted. That was before the letter came. But now I fear I hardly feel up to a tea party. I thought you could see the mine and then take the cake home with you when you go."

"Couldn't you tell us what's the matter?" said James. "Maybe we could help."

"Oh, I hardly think so," said Miss King, "though it is most kind of you. We must not burden others with our troubles."

"But we'd *like* to know," said Lydia. "That's if we're not butting in."

"Oh, not at all," said Miss King. "You are very thoughtful children. And here I am, keeping you on the doorstep. What would Pa say if he were here? Come in, come in!"

She ushered them into a tiny parlor that was so crammed with antiques and bric-a-brac the five of them could hardly fit in.

"You see," she went on when all were seated (James and Kip balanced precariously on the edges of their chairs lest they brush against some cherished heirloom), "you see, there is a thing called a mortgage."

"Yes, we know," said Laura. "We just bought a house."

"Then you know," said Miss King, "that it means paying a certain sum of money to the bank every month. And I have not been able to keep up the payments on mine. I have tried, but I had not a great deal of capital. There was a . . ." She paused and seemed reluctant to go on. "There was a misfortune many years ago. A large amount of money went out of the family . . . was lost, you might say. And little by little what was left has drained away. And now they write that they are going to foreclose."

"What does that mean?" said Kip.

"It means," said Miss King, "that they will take my home away. And where will I go? And what will I do?"

"Oh," said Kip.

"Couldn't you go to the bank and talk to them?" said James.

Miss King firmed her lips. "No," she said, "I could not. I have known Hiram Bundy since we were young together, though we have not spoken for many years. He is a just but hard man, and in this case justice is on his side."

"It would be!" burst out Lydia indignantly. "I *hate* cold, hard things like justice and banks and business and money!"

"So did I, my dear," said Miss King, smiling, "always. And see to what a pass it has brought me. You should profit from my example. But how depressing this must be for you, when what you really want is to explore the dear old mine and have your adventure! You'll find it just beyond the barn and through the gate. Forgive me if I do not accompany you. It would bring back memories of happier days!" And she touched her handkerchief to her eyes.

The four children filed solemnly out of the house

and across the yard and past the barn and through the gate in the old stone wall. They stood looking down at the Kingdom Mine.

You all know what an abandoned silver mine looks like, and this one was no different from any other, except perhaps a little smaller.

"It's just a hole in the ground!" said Lydia, disappointed. "It's just a ratty old hole!"

"It looks like any old gravel pit," said Kip.

"Maybe there's a Psammead buried in the bottom," said Laura, not very hopefully, "like in *Five Children and It*. And we could dig it out and make it wish the mortgage unforeclosed."

"Ha!" said James. "Not very likely! You and your old magic! You were so sure this was going to be a wonderful adventure and what do we get? Doom and gloom!"

Actually the Kingdom Mine was a perfectly good abandoned silver mine, and at any other time the four children might have found it an ideal spot for hiding in, and exploring, and getting thoroughly begrimed and blissful. But today they were too concerned about Miss King and her mortgage to think of anything else. And the sun went behind a cloud to sympathize with their mood.

Laura, as usual, was the first to get over being depressed and start trying to *do* something about it.

"I don't care," she said. "There is *so* magic! You

know how in the stories there're always tasks to do and quests to go on! Well, nowadays there wouldn't be dragons and princesses and witches; it'd be in modern guise, more! The magic sent her to us and it sent *us* to her! I feel it in my bones! We're supposed to *help* her!"

"What could we do?" said Kip.

"I don't know," said Laura. "Maybe the mine *isn't* played out and we could all get shovels and start digging and find silver and make it pay."

"I don't think silver pays very well any more," said James.

"Why not?" said Lydia. "People will always buy knives and forks!"

"I think it got kind of debased," said James, "when we went on the gold standard."

"What's that?" said Kip.

"I'm not sure," said James, "but it was bad for silver. There was a lot of fuss about it. Something about not crucifying mankind on a cross of gold. I read it in a book. But we went on it, anyway. Then just lately, we went off it again."

"Wasn't that *good* for silver?" said Kip.

"I don't think so," said James. "I think maybe we went on something else. Paper, maybe. No, I think silver's a thing of the past. *I* think the thing to do is go see that man in the bank. That Hiram Bundy."

And all agreed that that was the only proper course.

"I can't wait," said Lydia grimly.

But all agreed, too, that first they had better stay and play in the old silver mine awhile, just for the look of things and not to disappoint Miss Isabella.

And, as so often happens, once they forced themselves to pretend they were having fun, they began to *have* it, and the sun came out from its cloud, and Kip slipped and slid halfway down the shaft on the seat of his trousers, and Lydia nearly broke her neck when the eighty-second step in an old rotting wooden staircase she was counting (and climbing) broke through under her, and Laura found a rock that had a piece of what she was sure was silver in it, only James said it was probably only mica. And all in all, utter pleasure and oblivion prevailed, and it was only the voice of hunger that spoke at last and reminded them of Miss Isabella.

They trooped back to the house. On the porch an appetizing sight awaited them.

A table was laid for four, with slices of cake on old Wedgwood plates and glasses of raspberry vinegar and a box tied with scarlet-and-yellow ribbons.

On the box was an envelope addressed, "To My Four Friends." James opened it and read:

> "DEAR CHILDREN,
>   Not wishing to be a 'wet blanket,' as the boys say, I have decided to 'absent me from felicity.' Eat heartily and enjoy yourselves. The other half of the cake is in the box.
>   Yours faithfully,
>   ISABELLA CONSTANTIA KING"

There was a silence, except for fork-and-plate sounds. Then James spoke rather muffledly. "Any woman who makes cake like this, a bank should be proud to support."

"She should be subdivided by the government," agreed Kip, only he was not sure he had quite the right word.

When the last crumb was eaten and the last wonderful vinegary dregs drunk, the two girls tiptoed into the house and washed the dishes as quietly as possible in the kitchen. There was no sign of Miss Isabella.

"Probably lying down," said Laura.

"With eau de cologne on her forehead," agreed Lydia.

Laura found a paper towel (a surprisingly modern note in that old-fashioned house) and with her trusty pencil wrote a note to leave on the kitchen table. The note said:

"DEAR MISS KING,
    The cake was scrumptious. Do not despair. All is not yet lost.
                    Yours faithfully,
                        LAURA LAVINIA MARTIN"

And then she and Lydia went outside where the boys were kicking pebbles along the grassy gravel of the road.

By the time the four children reached the bridge, the sun was already sinking in the west, and everyone agreed it would be folly to try to see the wicked banker that day.

"Oh-oh. And tomorrow's Saturday. Banks are closed," said Kip.

"What of it?" said James. "We'll go see him in his house. He must live *somewhere* in town, mustn't he?"

"That's right," said Lydia. "We'll beard him in his lair."

"Hiram Bundy," said Kip. "He sounds like a miser in a movie."

"Take that, Hiram Bundy!" said Lydia, making a pass with an imaginary sword.

And then they went by the general store and four more houses, and the red house came in sight. James and Lydia and Kip went running to vault the picket fence and hurry inside to look up Hiram Bundy in the phone book. But Laura lingered.

She went up to the wishing well. "I don't care if that other wish *was* fake," she told it. "I *know* there's magic. I can feel it working. And I'm not going to write out wishes from now on. You can hear me perfectly well. You could fix it all up about Miss Isabella's house if you just would. Why, I bet if you really tried, you could have that Mr. Hiram Bundy eating right out of her hand! So please, please help us help her."

She leaned closer and listened, but the well did not respond. Laura thought at least it might have gurgled.

"I'm counting on you," she told it sternly.

Then she ran into the house.

4. The Wicked Ogre

It turned out that Mr. Hiram Bundy lived way over on the other side of town, too far for walking in comfort but a mere trifle for a demon cyclist.

"Bikes it is, then!" said James. "Zero hour nine-thirty on the dot!"

And then all separated for the night, to make plans and practice angry threats and (Laura) to say over all the magic spells that she knew. She had tried to interest Lydia in working some more witchcraft with the plants in her grandmother's garden, but Lydia would have none of it.

"I don't want to talk about that," she said. Moreover, she wouldn't.

And there may have been something wrong with the spells Laura said, because the next morning after breakfast her mother and father announced that they were spending the day at an auction and Laura and James were to stay home and baby-sit with Deborah.

"We can't possibly! We've got an important mission!" said James. "Can't you take her along with you?"

"No, we can't," said their mother. "She'll get up on her chair and call out things, and the people'll think she's bidding, and the next thing we know we'll have bought something horrible!"

"Want to go to the auction and bid," said Deborah.

"You see?" said their mother.

So that is the way it was, and ten minutes later their mother and father went off in a cloud of dust, and ten minutes after *that* Kip and Lydia came pedaling up to the house to find James and Laura sitting in the back yard glumly watching Deborah play something incomprehensible with acorns and Dutchman's-pipe flowers from the vine that screened the back porch.

"What are you doing?" said Kip.

"Minding baby," said James bitterly. And they told the tragic news.

"Why not bring her along?" said Kip. "She might come in handy. She can soothe the wicked ogre with her baby hands."

"Wicked ogre," said Deborah, smiling, as though she were looking forward to it.

"It's too far for her to walk," said Laura, "and Mother won't let her ride handle bars."

"*I* know!" said Lydia. "I'll take her on my horse and the rest of you can hitchhike. That'll be even quicker."

"Horse," said Deborah enthusiastically.

"We're not allowed to ride with strangers, either," said James, still sunk in gloom.

"They won't be strangers." Kip was scornful. "I know everybody in town, just about. It'll be a good way for you to meet your neighbors. It'll be useful and instructive."

So Lydia biked furiously home to change mounts. She was wearing a dress today instead of her usual old riding breeches, and Kip was in slacks and a sports shirt. So while she was gone, James and Laura changed into their best clothes in honor of the occasion. But they'd only been living in the country three days, and their best clothes were somewhat stiff and citified. Still, so much the better, thought James. Misers' houses were probably stiff and citified places.

They were hardly finished changing when Lydia came galloping back.

"Does your horse have a name?" said Laura, wanting to think of it as a friend and not a savage beast.

Lydia shrugged. "Why bother? It's not like a person. I told you, it's just a means to an end. It's just a horse."

"Horse," said Deborah again, reaching up to it lovingly.

So Lydia lifted her onto the horse's neck, while Laura shuddered and turned away.

But the horse seemed to like Deborah, and its evil eye turned kindly, and Deborah put her arms round its neck and crowed with delight.

"I'm afraid she's born to the saddle," said Lydia. "I'm afraid she's one of those girls that horseback-riding's going to be her whole life. Like those goons at the riding stable."

The other half of the cake Miss Isabella had given them was still in its box with the yellow-and-scarlet ribbons, and it was James who suggested they take it with them and present it to Mr. Hiram Bundy as a peace offering.

"If he gives in," he said, "it'll be his just reward, and if he doesn't, it'll be heaping coals of fire."

And so they started out, twenty minutes late but with hopes high.

The hitchhiking proved to be more hiking than hitching at first, because all the cars that went by either Kip didn't know or they had no room for three. And James's and Laura's stiff, citified clothes began to feel hot and scratchy. It was James who tore his jacket on a thorn and it was Laura who stepped into a bog in her best shoes.

Lydia walked her steed alongside and made conversation for a time, while Deborah called "Get a horse!" at them every few minutes derisively and laughed and laughed. But then Deborah decided she wanted to gallop and was so insistent that Lydia gave in, and they went rocking on far ahead.

And at last the other three got a ride as far as town with a woman Kip knew who told them all about a cake sale the Methodist Church was giving in aid of indignant widows (or it sounded like that). And that was useful and instructive.

In the town they found Lydia and Deborah. Lydia had tied her horse to a lamppost and they were both eating strawberry ice cream cones. It was Deborah who had spilled her cone down her front.

Naturally then, the others had to have mid-morning sustenance, too. They stood on the curbstone silently licking and dripping the ends of their cones into the gutter. Several of the passing motorists did not seem to appreciate Lydia's horse's taking up a parking place.

"It's that crazy Green girl," one woman was overheard to say. "Just running wild all over town. Somebody ought to do something!"

At this Lydia's face darkened, and she threw the rest of her cone away—but carefully, into a trash can. "Let's go," she said. So they did.

This time Kip and Laura and James got a ride with a man Kip knew who sold paper clips and stapling machines to the stationery store. He did not seem to want to talk about paper clips or anything else.

He set them down at the corner of Chickadee Drive, which was the street Mr. Hiram Bundy lived on, at number eighteen. Lydia and Deborah were already waiting at the corner.

"Chickadee Drive!" said James, as they went up it. "That doesn't sound like a mean old miser. He ought to live in Wolfpit Hollow!"

"Crooked Lane," said Laura.

"Skunk Street," said Kip.

Lydia didn't say anything.

Number eighteen, when they came to it, didn't look particularly like a mean old miser's house, either. It was a perfectly ordinary contemporary colonial split-level ranch house, just like any other, except maybe bigger and richer. An immense lawn surrounded it, with lots of shrubs clipped to look like other things than shrubs.

Lydia silently tied her horse to a tree by the road, and they went up the walk.

A nondescript woman answered their ring. "Well?" she said, looking at Laura's muddy feet dirtying the mat.

"We want to see Mr. Bundy," said James.

"Why?" said the woman.

"It's a business matter," said James.

"It's a matter of life and death," said Kip, at the same time.

"It's a life-and-death business matter," said Laura.

"Mr. Bundy is very busy. I doubt if he's at home," said the woman. "Summer people," she added, under her breath, contemptuously.

"We're not either! We all own our own homes!" cried Kip, outraged.

"Newcomers! Commuters!" muttered the woman, disappearing from view.

While she was gone, Laura tried to clean off Deborah's strawberry-ice-cream front with her handkerchief, but she only made it worse. Then she didn't know where to put the creamy handkerchief. She was hiding it behind a potted plant on the porch when the woman came back and eyed her suspiciously.

"He can give you three minutes. Follow me," she said.

The five children followed her stiff back through a hall and into a big study or library. Mr. Hiram Bundy was seated behind a huge desk that was covered with papers. Laura couldn't decide whether he looked like a mean old miser or not. His eyes were shrewd but his mouth was not unkind.

"Well?" he said, only half looking up from his papers. "If it's banking business, banking hours are on weekdays. If you wish to open an account, you must be accompanied by a parent or guardian."

"It's not that," said James. He hesitated. "It's kind of hard to begin," he admitted sheepishly.

Mr. Hiram Bundy put down his papers. His eyes traveled over them all slowly, taking in Deborah's strawberry front and not missing James's torn jacket and Laura's muddy shoes.

"If you are begging," he said briskly, "I do all my giving through organized charities."

This was more than Laura could stand. "We're not beggars . . ." she began. But she was interrupted.

Lydia had pushed forward and was looking at a big picture in a goldish frame that hung behind Mr. Bundy's desk. "Why, you've got one of my grandmother's pictures," she said.

Mr. Hiram Bundy's expression changed. "You are Agatha Green's granddaughter?"

"Yes I am," said Lydia defiantly. "I'm Lydia Green."

"Dear me," said Mr. Bundy. "I had no idea. Do be seated, all of you." He could not have been more cordial. "Your grandmother," he went on to Lydia, "is a remarkable woman. Without exaggeration I think I may say one of America's truly *great* women. She paints a maple tree as I've seldom seen it painted!"

At these words Kip looked at Laura and giggled, but not out loud.

"Now then," said Mr. Hiram Bundy, "what may I have the pleasure of doing for you?" And he beamed around at them all.

It was this moment that Deborah chose to very nearly spoil everything. She trotted forward and looked at Mr. Bundy. Then she turned to the others. "Wicked ogre!" she said, pointing at him and grinning from ear to ear.

The smile left Mr. Bundy's face. "What's that?" he said. "What was that?"

Throwing precaution to the winds, Laura stepped forward. Now that Deborah had gone that far, she might as well go the whole way.

"She called you a wicked ogre," she said, "because that's exactly what you are! How can you bear to foreclose Miss Isabella's mortgage and leave her with no home and nowhere to go?" She broke off, her cheeks crimson.

"I see," said Mr. Bundy. He did not sound angry, only concerned and regretful. "I understand your indignation," he went on, "and it does you credit. I have known Miss Isabella King for many years, though we have not spoken recently. Believe me, I respect her as much as you evidently do. But she is elderly and, if you will forgive me, no longer in full possession of her faculties. . . ."

James had had enough of this. He stepped forward and put the cakebox with its yellow-and-scarlet ribbons on Mr. Bundy's desk. "Just taste that cake," he said.

Mr. Bundy looked at him grimly. "Are you giving me orders, young man?"

"Just taste it," said James. He was deadly serious.

Mr. Bundy looked down at the cakebox. Something about the yellow-and-scarlet ribbons seemed to strike a chord. He undid them slowly, opened the lid, and looked at the cake. He crumbled off a corner and nibbled. Then he broke off a larger piece and chewed. Then he raised his voice.

"Mrs. Cheeseman!" he called.

The nondescript housekeeper appeared.

"Taste that cake," said Mr. Bundy.

"Oh, Mr. Bundy!" said the housekeeper.

"Taste it," said Mr. Bundy.

The housekeeper tasted it gingerly.

"Notice the texture?" said Mr. Bundy. "Moist, spongy, a bit of substance to it and yet not heavy? And not powdery and dry or bodiless fluff, either!"

"Very nice, I'm sure," said the housekeeper with a sniff.

"Very nice. Very nice," mocked Mr. Bundy. "I tell you, *there's cake!* Now go back to your kitchen and throw away your nasty soulless ready-mixes and cut yourself a real slice of that and eat it slowly and *study* it! And save me the rest for supper. That will do."

The housekeeper withdrew, bearing the cakebox and giving the five children a look as she passed.

"Well?" said James. "Would you say that a woman who can bake a cake like that was in full possession of her faculties or not?"

Mr. Bundy cleared his throat. "To be sure," he said. "Miss Isabella always had a light hand with a cake. From a girl. But there are other factors to be considered. She has been growing more and more eccentric of late, I hear. I am afraid it runs in the family. She had an aunt who became very peculiar in her old age. Very peculiar indeed. That was many years ago. But now they say Miss Isabella is going the same way. Consider her mode of dressing, for one thing. And her manner of speech has grown quite fantastic at times, they tell me. And then there is that old horse-and-buggy, getting in the way of traffic. Frankly, there have been complaints. Please believe me that this is no mere matter of money. The bank could afford to let the payments slip. And certainly Miss Isabella will not be homeless. Some suitable place will be provided for her. A convalescent home, perhaps."

"Do you think she'd like that?" said James. "What she wants is to be in her own house, with her own things."

"And her own silver mine," said Laura.

"Ah yes, that old mine," Mr. Bundy smiled sadly. "There have been complaints about that, too. Certainly it is an eyesore, if not actually a danger to the neighborhood children . . ."

"*We* played in it and *we* survived!" said Kip.

"No." Mr. Bundy shook his head decisively. "I am afraid that from all the evidence we must conclude that

Miss Isabella is no longer mentally capable of conducting her own affairs. Of living, in a word, her own life. And so it is with a clear conscience, though with genuine regret, that we have been forced to come to this decision. The place must be sold."

Lydia had not spoken for some time. Now suddenly she burst into speech, and, once started, it did not seem as if she would ever stop.

"You make me sick," she said. "You make me sick. Just 'cause my grandmother paints pictures that you like, you don't care what *she* does or how strange *she* goes around looking! I tell you, *our* house is twice as fallen down as Miss Isabella's, and *we're* not *poor!* But oh no, *that's* all right, 'cause Granny's a genius! I'm not saying she isn't. But what about other people who *aren't* geniuses and remarkable women of America and just don't happen to like everything everybody else likes and just want to go on living their lives in their own way? Oh, I *bet* you've had complaints! You've prob'ly had complaints about *me*, too! 'That crazy Green girl. Why doesn't somebody *do* something?' What *I* say is, why don't people mind their own business and leave us alone?"

She stopped, not because she had finished but because something seemed to get in the way of her going on. She turned and looked out the window. Her shoulders seemed to be shaking. Laura ran to her and threw her arms around her. Lydia tried to shake her off, but Laura was tenacious and would not be shaken.

James and Kip looked at the floor. Mr. Hiram Bundy got up from his chair. "There, there," he said, almost absently. "There, there."

There was a silence. Mr. Bundy walked up and down the carpet. When he spoke, it was in a low voice. "There may be something in what you say," he said. "I confess you have put the matter to me in a new light, though I can hardly take the responsibility . . ." He broke off. "What am I saying? Of *course* I can take the responsibility!" He straightened his shoulders. "I *will* take the responsibility! I shall tell the board tomorrow morning, and they can like it or lump it!"

Lydia turned from the window. She did not meet his eyes. But she said, "Thanks."

James held out his hand in a manly way. "Sir," he said, "you won't regret this decision."

"Then it's all right?" said Laura.

"You may tell your friend," said Mr. Hiram Bundy, "that she may disregard the letter from the bank and remain as she is, at least for the time being."

"Oh!" Laura beamed at the others. "Isn't it wonderful? The magic worked!"

"Yes," said Mr. Bundy, sitting at his desk again. "I guess it did."

Deborah had been sitting on the floor playing one of

her mystic games with the pattern of the library carpet and some pennies she'd found in her pocket. Now she seemed to sense a change in the atmosphere and looked up and around the room. "Isn't the ogre wicked any more?" she said.

"No," said Mr. Bundy from his chair, "he is thwarted."

"Oh." Deborah looked thoroughly disappointed. Then she trotted over to where Mr. Bundy sat and put out her hand and touched his cheek. "Poor," she said.

Kip giggled and whispered to Laura. "She's soothing the ogre with her baby hands!"

"Shush," said Laura. It was too solemn a moment.

"And now," said Mr. Bundy, eying James's jacket and Laura's shoes again, "since you seem to have had rather a desperate journey getting here, perhaps I can offer you a lift home in my car?"

"Do you drive fast?" said Laura.

"Yes," said Mr. Bundy with considerable zest, "I do. Will you come?"

Deborah drew herself up to her full height proudly. "*They* can," she said, "but *I* have my *horse!*"

And so it was that a few minutes later the town was startled by the sight of Mr. Hiram Bundy's commodious sedan fairly zooming along, with Lydia and Deborah galloping behind it, all the way down Elm Street.

"It's that crazy Green girl," said a woman passer-by.

"She is actually *chasing* poor Mr. Bundy's car. Somebody ought to do something!"

When they got back to the red house, first of course there was hunger to be placated (jam sandwiches and milk) and then of course all thoughts turned to Miss Isabella King and breaking the good news to her.

Deborah had only with difficulty been pried from the horse long enough to take nourishment, and now naturally she had to ride to Miss King's. But Lydia walked the horse all the way on this trip, for everybody had far too much to say to everybody else for them to be separated for a moment.

Magic was the burden of Laura's song. "*Now* do you believe?" she kept saying.

"I don't know," James told her finally. "It seemed to me what Lydia said had a lot to do with it. That was some speech, kid."

"Forget it," said Lydia gruffly.

"It was a wonderful speech," said Laura. "But maybe it was the magic that helped her say it."

"Rave on," said James.

"Mr. Bundy knew there was magic working," said Laura. "He admitted it."

"Maybe he was just humoring the village idiot," said James.

They had crossed the bridge now and come to the fork in the road. There was a black sedan parked by the turnoff, and Laura thought it looked familiar. The others seemed too busy puffing up the twisty, dusty, winding trail to notice, and Laura held her peace. After all, one black sedan was very much like another. And if she was right, it was more evidence to store up.

But when they reached Kingdom House, voices were heard coming from the parlor window. "I knew it!" said Laura, aloud.

"Shush," said James.

With one accord the five children tiptoed to the porch and peeked in. Mr. Hiram Bundy sat in the tiny parlor, balanced precariously on the edge of a chair with an empty Wedgwood plate balanced precariously on his knee. Miss Isabella King sat opposite him, pouring tea. Her face was wreathed in smiles, and the children knew somehow that their good news did not need to be broken.

"Your temper does not seem to have improved with the passing years, Hiram," Miss Isabella was saying.

"Dang it, Isabella, I'm still out of breath," said Mr. Bundy. "Why *will* you insist on living off on a rocky crag where a decent car can't penetrate? Curse and blast it, I have to consider my springs!"

"At *your* age, Hiram," said Miss Isabella sweetly, "I should think you would. Have another slice of cake."

As Laura watched Mr. Bundy take the slice of cake from Miss Isabella, she suddenly gasped (noiselessly) and made excited signs to the others. They all tiptoed off the porch again and ran to the brink of the silver mine, James taking care that Deborah didn't fall.

The others sat on the edge and dangled their legs over, while Laura walked up and down in her excitement and told them.

"It *is* magic. I know it now," she said. "I didn't tell you. Last night I wished on the well. And I said I wanted Mr. Bundy to eat out of Miss Isabella's hand. And you saw what just happened. That proves it."

"Unless it's a quincidence," said Kip.

James thought this over. "I guess it's too much of a one," he said. "I guess maybe there *is* magic, in a way."

"Of course it's 'in a way,' " said Laura. "It's *modern* magic. It would have to move with the times like anything else, wouldn't it? The way I figure is, it has to be unselfish. Modern magic is doing good turns to people. Only they always come out right—that's where the magic comes in. Those first wishes didn't work because they were selfish. Then the magic gave us another chance when it sent Miss Isabella. And we came through!"

"Gee!" said Kip. "If that's right, we can go on helping people right and left, all summer! We can hold the whole town in the hollow of our hand! We can do good turns to *everybody!*"

"Whether everybody likes it," said Lydia, a bit grimly, "or not!"

"We little know," said Laura, "the power we wield!"

"We can be malevolent despots!" said Kip.

"This," said James, "will take some thinking out. Let's go back to the house and think right now."

The five children got up and started away from the mine. They had got as far as the barn when Laura stopped. "Wait," she said. "Look!"

Mr. Bundy and Miss Isabella had come out onto the porch. Mr. Bundy was bending over in a low bow.

"What's he doing," said Kip, giggling, "biting the hand that fed him?"

"No," said Laura, rapt. "He's *kissing her hand!*"

Another moment and Mr. Bundy went tramping down the twisty trail and Miss Isabella went back inside. She appeared to be singing to herself.

"Well?" said Laura. "Has everybody seen enough? Shall we go home?"

"Horse," said Deborah happily.

5. The Long-Lost Heir

"How'll we get organized?" said Kip next morning,
as the four children sat under the apple tree behind the
red house. "Shall we go out and hunt for the magic or
let the magic come to *us*?"

Everybody looked at Laura. After all she was the
one who had realized there *was* magic in the first place.

"Well," said that priestess of the unseen slowly,
wrinkling her forehead, "I don't see that it much matters. I think we ought to just go about our daily life and
keep our eyes peeled for when opportunity knocks.".

"Good," said James. "Then let's go explore that river. I've always wanted to track one to its source."

But the others rejected this. "What good turns could we do *there?*" said Lydia scornfully. "We don't want to waste our magic on mere *beavers!* Let's go where there're people."

And all agreed that town was where there were the most of these.

"Ought we to speak to the well first?" Kip wondered, as they went down the path to the gate.

"How can we till we know what we want to wish?" said Lydia.

"We might drop it a hint," said Kip.

Laura paused by the wellhead. She looked down sternly at the mysterious depth below. "You know," she told it meaningfully. And they started up the road.

The first part of their journey was unproductive. All they met were a milkman who seemed quite happy in his work and sundry squirrels who appeared equally well adjusted. And the houses they passed looked serene and untroubled under the morning sun.

"Maybe we ought to start ringing doorbells," said James. "Maybe we ought to have a door-to-door campaign. *Somebody* must have a problem!"

Laura shook her head. "It'll come when it comes. You can't force it."

A man came walking down the road toward them,

and the four children quickened their steps. Maybe now the adventure would start.

But the man's face, as he came nearer, was wreathed in smiles and he swung a hickory stick jauntily. "What weather!" he cried. "Glorious. Up at six. Did three miles already. Mean to do three more. Makes you glad to be alive, doesn't it?"

"Sure, I guess it does," said Kip, rather dispiritedly.

"No good we can do *him*," said James, when the man had passed.

"Not a care in the world," agreed Lydia bitterly.

A car slowed up beside them and a woman looked out. "Want a ride? Hop in," she said. So they hopped in. Maybe this time opportunity would really knock.

But the woman's face was plump and jolly and her voice had the ringing tones of utter optimism. "Isn't it a glorious day?" she said. "So cool for July!"

"Here we go again," muttered James to Lydia. " 'What weather! Makes you glad to be alive!' "

The woman had overheard. "It certainly does!" she cried. "You took the words right out of my mouth!"

"Don't despair," muttered Lydia to the others. "Maybe she wears a painted smile to hide a breaking heart." She raised her voice. "But don't you sometimes feel," she said, "that it's all a mockery? When you've got troubles down inside, doesn't a wonderful day like this make you feel *worse?*"

"It certainly doesn't!" said the woman. "Times I feel like that, I just jump in my little car, throw out the clutch, and away I go!"

And she suited the action to the words, zooming along the road blowing her horn and waving at the other motorists and now and again singing snatches of song, "I Love Life" and "Let a Smile Be Your Umbrella."

"Whew!" said James, when the enthusiastic woman had finally set them down at the corner of Main and Elm.

" 'You took the words right out of my mouth,' " quoted Kip, giggling.

"The trouble with this town," said Lydia, "is that everybody's too darned *happy!* Nobody needs a helping hand at all."

It may have been that the magic overheard these hapless words and took its revenge. Or, as Kip said afterwards, it may have been a quincidence.

But hardly had he and Laura and Lydia and James taken three steps down Main Street when a voice hailed them.

"Oh, children!" were its insulting words.

Kip and Laura and Lydia and James looked up and down the street. No children seemed to be in sight.

"Oh, children!" said the voice again, and this time there was no mistaking whom it meant. A woman was standing in the door of the art supply store, looking straight at them. Her arms were piled high with framed masterpieces. "Children," said the woman for the third time, "I am in charge of arranging the pictures for the sidewalk art show and my team hasn't showed up. I know you won't mind helping. It's a civic project."

"Oh," said James and Kip and Lydia and Laura.

"You boys can just carry these screens around and space them by the curbstone," said the woman, "and the girls can help me hang the pictures."

"What's it all in aid of?" said James, who had heard this phrase somewhere.

"Why, it's to encourage our local amateur artists!" said the woman. "I guess we'll show people our town's got talent! Anybody can enter and just about everybody *has!*"

As the four children surveyed the crowded interior of the art store, it did indeed look as if this were true. There were forty of the big, heavy screens for James and Kip to place strategically along Main and Elm Streets, and each screen could display six pictures.

And as Laura and Lydia and the women dealt with these, Laura began to feel that perhaps too many local artists had been encouraged. Some of the pictures were good, but there were the usual woolly landscapes and studies of squinting sinister Arabs and stalwart Indian chiefs. And there were others so modern and strange that Laura and the woman couldn't decide which way was up and which way was upside down. But somehow Lydia always knew.

And so the morning wore on and the sun grew hotter, and perspiration dewed each brow, and the magic didn't see fit to come to their aid or make the minutes go by any faster. By the time the tardy members of the woman's team arrived to take over, nearly two hours had passed, and James and Kip and Laura and Lydia agreed that it was time to cheer their flagging spirits with hot butterscotch sundaes.

Kip and Lydia led the way to the other drugstore, not the best one nor the fairly good one, but the old one that hardly anybody ever went into any more. Kip felt sorry for it because its interior was dim and dingy and fly-haunted, and Lydia liked it because it had old bottles of red and green water in the windows and the woman clerk always acted so surprised when any customers came in at all.

"Honestly, some of those pictures!" said Laura ten minutes later, licking the last strings of butterscotch from her spoon. "Why, any of us could do one as good as *those!*"

"Let's!" said Kip.

Everybody looked at everybody else.

"She said anyone can enter," said James. "Who are we to be behindhand?"

There was an investigating of pockets. James and Laura had twenty-seven cents between them, and Kip, who had treated them all to the sundaes, had the change left over from two dollars (money he had earned mowing lawns). Lydia had nothing at all.

Altogether there was enough to buy a drawing pad and a box of crayons, and the reluctant woman clerk was summoned again from the dark beyond where she preferred to stay.

After that there was concentrated silence for a while, but then James and Kip began looking over each other's shoulders and snickering and pushing each other's elbows and at last crumpled their papers up and announced that they couldn't draw for nuts.

"It's harder than it looks," James admitted.

Laura persisted for a while. She had a marvelous scene in mind, blue sky and green trees and white houses, all fresh and new-washed, the way they had looked early that morning when she had come along the road, but somehow the crayons refused to cooperate. And no magic touch came to guide her faltering hand, either. At last she too crumpled up her picture and looked idly across the table at Lydia's. Then she looked again.

Lydia had used only the black crayon, and at first what she had done seemed like just a lot of meaningless lines and curves, but when Laura looked a second time, she saw that the curves were eyes and that the picture was dozens and dozens of pairs of eyes that seemed to be looking straight at her and that somehow added up to form a pattern and even seemed to say something, though Laura wasn't sure just what.

The others were looking at Lydia's picture now, too.

"That's good," said James judicially.

"No it isn't," said Lydia.

"I didn't know you could draw," said Kip.

"I can't. It's just doodling," said Lydia. She made as if to crumple up her paper like the others.

"Don't!" said Laura, snatching it away.

And then the drawing was forgotten (for the moment) as they all pushed back their chairs and got up, and Kip knocked a nickel against the glass counter-top to lure the woman clerk from her inner fastness. He paid for the art materials, and the four children started for the door. And it was then that they found the long lost heir.

"Aren't you forgetting your little brother?" said the woman.

James and Kip and Laura and Lydia looked around. The woman did not stay for an answer but retreated into the gloom at the rear.

It was Lydia who saw the little boy first. He was a very little boy and he was sitting silent and contented on the floor in a far corner of the store, playing with a celluloid pinwheel.

"Well, for heaven's sake!" said Lydia. "Are you lost?"

"Lost," said the little boy contentedly.

Lydia went up to him. "Can't you find your mother?"

"Mother," said the little boy, throwing his arms possessively round one of Lydia's legs and beaming up at her angelically.

"Aw!" said Lydia, her iron soul melting.

"He *is* lost," said Laura.

"Or strayed," said Kip.

"We'd better take him to the police station right away," said James.

"No!" cried Laura. "Don't you see? It's the magic working at last! It's our good turn for today. It must be. We're supposed to find him and take him home *by ourselves!*"

James was studying the little boy. "He's dressed awful fancy," he said. "He's probably the long-lost heir to untold millions."

"Only the richest velvet is allowed to touch his satin skin," said Kip, giggling.

"Exactly!" said Laura. "We'll restore him to his sorrowing parents and earn priceless rewards!" She lowered her voice. "He's probably been kidnaped and held for ransom. This place is probably a thieves' den in disguise! It *looks* like it! That's probably why they never seem to want any customers!"

And the others agreed that this was only logical.

"But the woman wanted us to take him," objected Kip.

"She's probably the kidnaper's downtrodden wife, like Nancy Sikes," said Laura. "She was probably feeling remorseful. She might change her mind any minute and betray us to the gang! We've got to get out of here! Come on!"

"Come on!" repeated James, chirping encouragingly at the little boy.

"Carry," said the little boy, holding up his arms trustingly.

"Oh!" cried Lydia, melting again. She scooped the little boy up in her arms and held her cheek against his. "Oh, tweety wee swummy doodle!"

James and Kip looked away in disgust. Laura marveled. She would never have recognized Lydia in this guise.

But this was no time to be standing here marveling. "Hurry!" she breathed. And the four children stole out of the drugstore (or kidnapers' den), Lydia carrying the long-lost heir.

Once in the everyday light of Main Street, things didn't seem quite so perilous, and Laura remembered something.

"Wait here," she said. "I have to go straighten that last picture I hung."

"Honestly!" said Kip. "At a time like this!"

"Psst," James hissed in his ear, and gave him a meaningful look. The two boys squinted across Main Street at the art store and watched what Laura did. Lydia was too busy exchanging endearments with the little boy to notice.

"There," said Laura a second later, rejoining them.

"Now what?" said Kip.

"Back to the wishing well, I'd say," said James, "and bring it up to date, just to make sure."

So they turned their steps toward Silvermine Road.

Luckily a woman offered them a lift before they'd gone a block, and as luck would have it, it was the same optimistic woman who had brought them into town that morning. Now she proved to be not only optimistic but inquisitive.

"Well! Something new has been added!" she cried enthusiastically. "Is that your baby brother?"

"Brother," said the little boy contentedly, and the four children did not correct him. If that was the way the magic wanted it to be, so be it.

"Where'd you find him?" went on the woman.

"He was waiting in the drugstore," said Laura. After all, that was perfectly true.

The woman set them down at the red house, and Laura was first to reach the wishing well.

"We found the long-lost heir all right," she told it. "Now let us get him back to his ancestral acres and earn the reward."

The wishing well gave its usual reply (silence).

"What next?" said Kip. "How do we know where to take him?"

"Why not ask him?" said Lydia.

"That's right," said James. "We never thought of that."

The four children formed a circle round the long-lost heir, who was sitting contentedly on the grass blowing his pinwheel.

"Where do you live?" asked Laura.

"Home," said the long-lost heir. And that was all they could get out of him.

"So much the better," said James. "Now it's up to the magic to show what it can do. He can play with Deborah in the meantime. Let's have lunch."

But when they went inside, it turned out that James and Laura's parents had gone to Stamford to another auction and taken Deborah with them. The note they had left went on to say that sandwiches were to be found in the refrigerator, and these, when scrupulously divided, made a frugal repast for five.

"And now," said James, "let's go explore that river. The magic'll find us wherever we are. No sense in sitting around waiting. A watched well's no better than a watched pot."

"What about *him?*" said Laura. "We can't leave him alone here and he'll be too heavy to carry."

"I don't mind," said Lydia in her newfound character of little mother.

"You won't have to," said Kip. "They've got an old

rowboat down at the tearoom that we can prob'ly hire.
I've still got fifty cents left."

And when they arrived at the tearoom (Lydia trun-
dling the heir in the garden cart), it turned out that the
people would gladly accept fifty cents down and the
rest on trust; so *that* was all right.

As the four children (and the heir) shoved off from
shore, the sound of a fire engine was heard in the distance, and James and Kip briefly regretted not being
on dry land and able to chase after it on their bikes.
But the sound died away in the distance and was soon
forgotten in the joy of watery exploration.

Under the bridge by the tearoom the river was narrow and trickly, and the boat bumped against rocks.
But around the first bend was a wide lakelike part edged
with waterlilies and dark with ducks that scattered before them, making the air sound with their wingbeats.
Kip shipped the oars and let the boat drift awhile. The
sun was warm and the water sparkled. Lilies were
picked and frogs caught and let go again. Perfect peace
was enjoyed by all. The long-lost heir slumbered in
Lydia's lap. Perhaps some others slumbered, too.

How many hours went by in soporific floating will
never be known. But James was not one to forget a
cherished goal for too long.

"Let's go," he said suddenly, stirring himself. " 'Out
of the hills of Habersham, down the valleys of Hall!' "

"Only we're not; we're going *up*stream," pointed out Kip practically.

James rowed for a while, but what Kip had said proved all too true, and he made small headway against the current, for now the river grew ever more deep-gorged and dramatic and rapids-y, and the rocks were big and sharp and hazardous. Around another bend a roaring waterfall appeared ahead, blocking their way.

"This is too much of a good thing," said James. "We'll have to portage."

He picked out a safe-looking landing spot and Lydia set the long-lost heir on the shore. That is how his trousers got muddy behind. The others clambered out after him, and James and Kip managed to get the boat out of the stream. They carried it while the girls went on ahead. At the waterfall everybody stopped and Kip showed the others how to walk behind it. That is how the long-lost heir's shirt got so wet.

But whatever comes down must have been up, and this is true of shore as well as water. So next to the waterfall were rocky heights to scale, and Laura helped the boys get the boat up these. Every once in a while Lydia had to help, too. When she did this, she set the heir down, and every time she did, he began to crawl. That is how he got muddy in front and lost a shoe.

All this took a long puffing time, but luckily there was a sunny clearing at the top and everybody collapsed with moans of languor and lay prone or supine

for a while, making desultory conversation. Everybody
except the heir. Having had no work to do, he was still
fresh as a daisy and crawled around them in a circle, inspecting the local plant and insect life. That is how he
got the mud on his face and the leaves in his hair.

Next to the clearing was a broad calm level stretch of
river, and it was James who got his breath back first and
suggested that they board the boat once more. This
time Lydia rowed. As she pulled away from the bank,
the others thought they heard a fire siren again, but the
noisy waterfall was still too near for them to be sure.

Ever and anon along their course the four children
had seen houses on the bank, comfortable country-ish
places surrounded by all the natural beauties of wood
and water. Now as they rounded the next bend, they
saw a house of another color.

Its color was pink, but that was not the only unusual
thing about it.

It was big and modern and low and glassy and no ex-
pense had been spared. There were greenhouses and
tool houses and summerhouses galore. No remnant of
the original woods had been allowed anywhere near it.
As for the river, it had been neatly dredged and made to
look as much like an artificial swimming pool as possible, with all the lovely natural rocks carted away.

Where the woods had once been, all was bland roll-
ing lawn and paved driveway. And in the driveway
were parked not one, not two, but three sports cars.

One was a Porsche, one was a Jaguar, and one was a wonderful new kind neither of the boys had ever seen before. They stared at it with the round eyes of utter car-worship.

"I've got to see this closer," said James. "Pull for the shore, sailor." And Lydia did.

There was a neat dock, of course, with a diving board. But as the boat drew alongside, a woman in a cap and apron came from the house and ran toward the dock, waving her arms in a fussy and henlike manner.

"Go away," she said. "No trespassing. This is private property."

"We're sorry," said Kip pleasantly. "We thought this was a public river."

"We thought we had riparian rights," added James.

"None of your big words!" said the woman. "The nerve! Nasty sight-seers, coming to spy on Madam in her grief. Morbid, I call it!"

"We're sorry," said Kip again. "We'll be going, right away."

At this moment the long-lost heir leaned out of the boat. "Fussy," he said.

"She certainly is!" said Lydia. "As if we'd hurt her old dock! Let's go."

But the woman on the dock was staring at the heir. "Master Harold!" she cried. "Found! Found at last! Come to Fussy!" And she held out her arms.

"Won't," said the long-lost heir, turning away.

"Wait a minute," said James. "Is this your nurse or something?"

For answer, the heir made a face and hid behind Lydia.

The four children hesitated. But the woman did not. She began waving her arms and screaming hysterically. "Kidnapers!" she cried. "McTavish! Call the men! Call the Madam! Set the dogs on them!"

A man came running with a rake. He gave a whistle and more men appeared, with two great Baskerville-looking hounds. The man with the rake caught the side of the boat and pulled it against the dock.

"You needn't bother," said Lydia, with frigid dignity. "I can land perfectly well."

But nobody heard her because quite a crowd had collected by now and everyone was talking (or barking) at once without seeming to make any sense whatever. The word "kidnapers" was frequently heard.

A richly dressed lady came running from the house and joined the group. She was just about the prettiest lady any of the four children had ever seen. As Kip said afterwards, movie stars weren't in it with her. And the girls agreed that that was putting it mildly.

But right now her lovely face was distorted with emotion, and sounds of a peacock-like nature issued from her marble throat as she beheld the boat and its contents.

"What have you done with my baby?" she cried.

The four children regarded the muddy, damp, leafy, one-shoe-off-and-one-shoe-on heir and had to admit in their minds that they might have returned him in better condition.

"They stole him!" cried the woman called Fussy before anyone else could answer. "Dirty, common children they are! They stole him while my back was turned!"

This was too much for Lydia. Dirty she might be, but common never. "The idea!" she said. "We saved him from a den of iniquity, that's all!"

"And brought him back to his ancestral acres," added Kip.

"By magical means," put in Laura.

"Your back must have been turned a good long while," said James. "We were in that drugstore twenty minutes at *least* and never saw hide nor hair of you."

"Oh, the horrid fibbers!" cried the Fussy woman. "I *may* have passed the time of day with a friend, but I wasn't gone thirty seconds."

At this everyone began talking at once again. The dogs, which as James put it later seemed more basking than Baskerville, added to the confusion by wreathing around people's legs, barking happily.

A man came up to the group. He was as handsome as the lady was beautiful and as richly dressed. At first his face looked drawn and worried, but as he listened it relaxed, and when he spoke, Laura thought she saw a smile starting at the corners of his eyes.

"Just a minute," he said. "I suggest we could discuss this better on dry land and indoors. And with only the immediate parties concerned present."

The child Harold was handed ashore, not without a determined struggle on his part to remain in the boat, and borne off an unwilling prey to the ministrations of the Fussy woman, though Laura thought the Fussy woman looked as if she would rather have stayed. The crowd of men dispersed, taking the dogs (still barking) with them, but first tying the boat to the dock. James and Laura and Kip and Lydia followed the lady and gentleman into the house and through a plant-ridden hall to the living room.

The living room was long and low and furnished in the finest chromium, with decorative pieces of driftwood sitting on all the tables.

"Sit down," said the father of the heir. "Begin at the beginning."

And Laura did, beginning farther back than James wished she would. She told all about the magic and the adventures so far and how they planned to spend all the rest of the summer doing good turns to everybody.

"Very interesting," said the man. "But if bringing my son home was your next good deed, may I point out that you might have done it with a little more dispatch? He has been missing for *eight hours!*"

"Oh dear," said Laura. "Has he?"

"Good grief!" said James. He turned to Kip. "And tonight's the night we're all due at your house for dinner! We'll be late."

"That," said the man, "can be arranged. But not yet. Go on. Tell me more."

"We've been just frantic!" said the lady, before James could. "We had the police out and the Volunteer Fire Brigade and everything!"

"We thought we heard sirens," said James, "but we were too busy to take much notice."

"You were too busy," said the man. "I see. Go on."

"It was even broadcast on the radio!" the woman interrupted again.

"And one interesting clue turned up," said the man. "A woman phoned us that she had given a lift to some children with a little boy. They *said* he was their little brother." And he looked at the four children.

"We let her think that," said Laura, "to save time."

"To save time," repeated the man. "Interesting. And what did you save the time *for*? What were you too busy *doing*? If I may ask." His tone was grim, but Laura did not think he was really very angry.

"We were tracking the river to its source," said James. "I guess we went to sleep for a while, too. And that's quite a climb along by the waterfall. It's a tough trip."

"Poor little baby!" said the mother of the heir. "He was just exhausted."

"Ahem," said her husband. "As to that, I cannot see that my son has suffered any irreparable harm. In fact, he seems to have enjoyed the whole thing thoroughly. I've no doubt a few more tough trips and a little less Fussiness (and here Laura could have sworn he winked at them) would do him a great deal of good. However" —and here his face became stern again—"I suggest that when you do your next good deed, you *finish* it before starting some other adventure. And when in doubt, ask a policeman." He relaxed. "And now, since the *long-lost* heir is at *last* returned to his sorrowing family, I should think a celebration is in order. What would you like?"

"We didn't do it for a reward," said James. "Not mainly."

"We did it for the glory of it," beamed Laura. "And to test the magic."

"But if you *do* want to do anything for us," said James, "a ride in that car would be dandy."

"Not the Jag or the Porsche but the other one," said Kip. "You could take us home and kill two birds with one stone."

"That," said the gentleman, "I was meaning to do anyway. However. We shall see. In the meantime, come along." He grinned at them.

The lady, too, managed a smile, but it was a pale and

wan one and her heart was not in it. You could see that
she was thinking of their muddy feet on her good rugs
(except that the floors were not carpeted, being all of
glossy imported imitation-marble tiling).

As for the boat, Kip said he thought he could bribe
the older boy next door to pick it up after dinner that
night in his family's station wagon; so all loose ends
were taken care of.

The strange and wonderful sports car proved to be
all that James or Kip could have desired. You would
not have thought that all four children and the man
could fit in, but somehow, what with laps and squash-
ing, this was managed. And luckily part of the road
home was straight and broad and un-trafficky and the
man could really let it out. The entire undertaking was
not much of a reward to Laura, but she shut her eyes
and bore it.

James was thoughtful as they walked up the path to
Kip's house (after saying good-by to the man and his
car). "I don't know," he said. "It seems to me the
magic could have done better. If there *is* magic."

"We're not going to start all that again, are we?" said
Laura. "Of course there's magic. It took us right there
to the heir's home, didn't it?"

"It *took* us there," said James. "But *right* there you
couldn't say. As far as I can see, all we did was make
the long-lost heir lost *longer*. He'd have been rescued
ages ago if we'd let well enough alone."

"But we had the fun of doing it," said Laura. "Anyway, maybe that drugstore *is* a thieves' den. Maybe something awful would have happened to him if he'd stayed there another minute."

"Or maybe the magic put him there in the first place," said Kip, "to teach us a moral lesson."

"Ugh!" said James.

"Anyway, you got your ride in your old sports car," pointed out Lydia.

"That's true," said James. "There *is* that."

Lydia was coming to dinner at Kip's house, too. It was Kip's mother's idea that all the families should get acquainted. Lydia's grandmother had been asked, but had declined.

And yet when the four children entered the living room, there was old Mrs. Green with the others. There seemed to be an air of excitement in the room, and all the parents and guardians were looking at the children in rather an odd way, as if they wondered what they would do next.

"Where have you been?" said Kip's mother. "We've been waiting and waiting. I suppose you've heard the news?"

"Oh, did you hear about it, too?" said Kip. "On the radio, I suppose. And the fire engines and all. Well, don't worry. It all ended fine."

"I don't know what you're talking about," said Kip's mother. "I meant about the sidewalk art show."

"What?" said Laura, remembering something.

And it turned out that her guess was right, because what she had done that morning when she ran across the street and pretended to straighten a picture was enter Lydia's drawing in the show, and it turned out that the judges had been very impressed by it and had given Lydia a special award for the most promising work by a student.

Lydia's first reaction when she heard was one of fury, which was typical.

She turned on Laura. "How dare you put that in without telling me?"

But Laura had known Lydia long enough now to be undisturbed by her wrath. "I just thought I would," she said airily. "I knew you never would yourself. You'd rather feel unappreciated and that nobody cares. But it's nice when you find out that you aren't and they do. Isn't it?"

"Yes," said Lydia after a minute. "I guess it is." But she still looked stunned. "They can't mean it," she said. "It was just doodling."

"Would," said her grandmother, "that I could doodle as well. Why didn't you ever tell me you could draw?"

"I didn't know I could," said Lydia. "If I can."

"You can," said old Mrs. Green. "Not that you don't have a lot to learn still. I suppose if I'd paid more attention, I might have guessed you had it in you. I'm a selfish old woman. Still, I suppose it's too late to change."

"Are you sure you won't stay for dinner?" said Kip's mother.

Old Mrs. Green looked for a minute as if she would almost like to. Then she shook her head. "I haven't dined out in years. No point in starting now. Thanks just the same. I'm a cantankerous curmudgeon and let's leave it at that." And she stumped away, looking more wild-haired and witchlike than ever.

Laura looked after her. It seemed to her that Lydia and her grandmother had a lot in common. Still, it was wonderful how the magic had brought Lydia out. Maybe if it got a chance, it could bring old Mrs. Green out, too, and smooth her down and brighten her up. Maybe it would be worth while *giving* it a chance and letting it try.

She came to herself to find everyone looking at her and laughing.

"What is it?" she said.

"Dinner is served," James told her. "Kip's mother just told you for the third time. Where've you been? Come on down to earth and let's eat."

And they did.

6. The Mob-led Queen

It was the next afternoon, as the four children were sitting by the wishing well planning what good deeds to perpetrate next, that James and Kip suddenly pricked up their ears ("just like a couple of old pointer dogs," as Lydia put it) at the magic sound of sports car upon the breeze. And the father of the long-lost heir came speeding round the bend and stopped at the gate in the picket fence.

"The rest of the reward," he told them, grinning, as they clustered round the car. And he handed out four small packages and wouldn't take no for an answer, but zoomed away before even Lydia could get her outside wrapping undone.

The four packages contained a gold wrist watch each, and the four children were suitably grateful. Moreover, they got the point.

After that, whenever they encountered the father of the heir in town, he would sing out, "What time is it?" and the four children always knew. But when he would go on to ask how the magic was coming, and when on another occasion they met Mr. Hiram Bundy and he asked the same thing, there was less to report.

The next few days were ordinary ones, as *will* sometimes happen in even the most magical of vacations. No further lost people were found, and no strangers came tapping at the door except a woman who wanted to know where the Butterworths lived and a boy who was working his way through college selling subscriptions to *The Saturday Evening Post.*

Laura was sure these might be more visitors from another world in disguise and wanted to follow them and see where the trail might lead, but James counseled against it.

"We don't want to start overreaching again," he said, "the way we sort of did last time. Let the magic take its course from now on. It'll let us know when it's ready."

But as the year turned on and July got to be August, Laura grew more impatient. The four children sat on the sun-warmed rocks at the foot of Kip's mother's rock garden one afternoon and discussed the situation.

"Don't worry," said Kip. "It's probably just building up to something big. This is probably just the calm before the storm."

"We want to keep on our toes, though," said Laura. "You never can tell when it'll strike. Look at that art show!"

"Honestly!" said James. "You give the magic all the credit! You wouldn't think maybe a little *talent* had something to do with it?"

"It took the magic to bring it out," insisted Laura. "Didn't it?" She turned to Lydia.

Lydia was a changed person these days. Wherever she went, she had a pencil in her hand and a drawing before her. If no pencil was handy, she used whatever *was*. Now she was tracing a design in the earth with a pointed stick.

"It's the knowing there's some point to it. That's the thing," she said after a minute. "In school, before, the kids always said, 'Why d'you draw such crazy pictures?' And the teacher was always telling me to paint from nature!"

"I know," said Kip sympathetically. "It's like when I try to write stories and they tell me to write what I know about! If I *knew* about it, what would be the point of *writing* it?" He broke off, as voices were heard from the garden above. "Oh glory!" he muttered. "I forgot. Mother has to show Mrs. Witherspoon the garden today. I meant to escape."

"Mrs. *Gordon T.* Witherspoon?" said Lydia. "Help!"

"Who's she?" said James.

"She's president of the Garden Club," said Kip, "and she's *horrible*."

"Ghastly," agreed Lydia.

"Why's she called Mrs. Gordon *T.* Witherspoon?" said Laura. "How many Mrs. Gordon Witherspoons are there?"

"One," said Kip, "is enough."

And as James and Laura peered up through greenery at Kip's mother's guest, they had to agree in their minds that one of her would be ample.

"My dear," Mrs. Gordon T. Witherspoon was saying, eying an inoffensive-looking plant with disfavor, "you don't grow *that*, do you? It's nothing but a pest!" And transfixing the plant with the point of her shooting stick, she dragged it from the earth, roots and all, and cast it upon the path.

Kip's mother's face grew pink and she pressed her lips together, but said nothing.

Mrs. Witherspoon went on stalking about the garden and criticizing its contents in a forthright and unabashed manner, while the four children scrooched down and hoped to escape notice. Either they did, or Mrs. Witherspoon was the type who thinks children

shouldn't be heard or seen either, for she treated their
presence with a marble disdain.

"Now maybe she'll go," whispered Kip, when Mrs.
Witherspoon had disparaged the entire garden.

But she didn't. She settled down on a garden seat as
though she proposed remaining there for some time.
"And now my dear," she said, "as to the real reason I
wanted to speak to you. It's about next week's town
meeting. We property owners must band together and
block that new school!"

Kip's mother's face grew pink and she pressed her
lips together again. But "What do you mean?" was all
she said.

"Why, my dear," said Mrs. Witherspoon, "hadn't
you heard? The town wants to build a great big new
school right here on this road! And you know what
that will mean! Children running over the lawns all
hours of the day; we won't have a minute's peace.
Think of the traffic! Those noisy buses. And *real estate
values*"—here her voice took on the important tone
of one who deals with a sacred subject—"will go
down!"

Kip's mother was looking really angry now. But "I
think we need a new school," was all she said.

"Let them build it somewhere else, then!" said Mrs.
Witherspoon grandly. "Though personally I don't see
the necessity. The more schools we have, the more people will want to move here, and we'll lose our lovely old

village quality. New York people," she added in tones of distaste.

"*I* came here from New York," said Kip's mother rather coldly.

"To be sure, my dear," said Mrs. Witherspoon, "but you've fitted in beautifully. No one would ever know. As a matter of fact, Mr. Witherspoon's people lived in Brooklyn Heights at one time. But that was years ago. It's this new element we want to discourage."

"That means us," muttered James to Laura.

Lydia threw them a loyal look, and Kip made a strangling motion in the direction of Mrs. Witherspoon.

Kip's mother was standing up now. But she kept her voice polite. "I'm afraid I don't agree with you at all, Mrs. Witherspoon," she was saying. "We need that new school and I'm going to fight for it as hard as I can. All my friends are, too."

"Well, my dear," said Mrs. Witherspoon grimly, surging to her feet, "you may find yourself in a very small minority. A very small minority indeed! Most of the responsible people in town generally agree with *me!*" And she stumped away toward the front gate and didn't even speak to Kip's father when he arrived home just then from his commuting train, though he raised his hat politely.

"Honestly, Fred," the four children heard Kip's mother saying to Kip's father a few minutes later, while he soothed her with a cooling cocktail, "I was so mad I could hardly see. She'll do it, too. She'll steam-roller that new school right out of existence, no matter what we do. Half the town follows her just like a flock of sheep!"

"And that's the truth," said Kip, as he and Laura and Lydia and James wandered away from the house and into the road. "Mrs. Witherspoon just about runs this whole neck of the woods."

"She's a regular old queen," said Lydia. "A regular old mob-led queen."

"What's that?" said James.

"It's Shakespeare," said Lydia. "It means she led the whole mob. I think."

"That's Mrs. Witherspoon!" agreed Kip.

"I hadn't heard about this school," said James. "Do we need it?"

"Yes," said Kip. "We do."

"Then let's do something," said James. "Let's get all *our* friends to come to town meeting and vote on our side."

"Who could we get?" said Kip practically (though ungrammatically).

"There's the long-lost heir's parents," said Laura.

"Summer people," said Kip. "And weekends. Probably never go to town meeting at all."

"There's Miss King." But even hopeful Laura could see that gentle Miss King would stand small chance against Mrs. Gordon T. Witherspoon.

"Mr. Hiram Bundy?" suggested James.

Kip shook his head. "He's a public figure. Probably has to stay nonpartisan."

And it was then that Laura saw their way clear before them. "Then I guess it's up to the magic," she said.

"That's right," said Kip. "I was forgetting for a minute."

"This could be the big thing it's been building up to," admitted James.

"You mean we could get it to work on Mrs. Witherspoon?" said Lydia.

"How?" said Kip. "Make an image of her and stick pins in it?"

"*No!*" cried Laura in horror. "That might make her *worse!* If she's the way she is now, think what she'd be like with shooting pains!"

Everybody did, and shuddered at the thought.

"We could make an image and be *kind* to it," said Lydia. "Like the children in *The Wonderful Garden.*"

"Sure," said Kip, "and soothe it and pet it and lay flattering unction to its soul!"

At the thought of soothing and petting an image that looked like Mrs. Witherspoon, all four gave way to giggles. Laura was the first to recover.

"No, don't you see?" she said. "That's exactly what we'll do, only we won't use any old image. We'll do it *directly*. To *her!*"

"You mean we could do her good turns," said James.

"And dance attendance on her and minister to her every wish," said Kip.

"Why not?" said Laura. "Then when she gradually gets used to us, she'll see how nice school children can be, and she won't mind having the school nearby at all!"

"I never thought," said Lydia, "that I'd ever go to any trouble for that old school!"

"But it won't be," said Kip. "It'll be a new one. Wait and see. Shall we start right now?"

"Better give her a chance to cool down," said James. "It's getting late, anyway. Better begin first thing in the morning."

"Let's go tell the well," said Laura.

And they went and told it in no uncertain terms.

The rest of that evening was spent in planning their campaign.

"We ought to go bearing gifts," said James. "Only what could we take? What have we got that she hasn't got?"

"I could bake my butterscotch brownies," said Laura. "Only she probably has scads of servants tempting her with tasty viands all day long."

"It's like picking out a Christmas present for some-body who has everything," said Lydia.

"I guess we'll just have to take her our own sweet selves," said Kip.

And in the end that is mainly what they did.

Only Laura *did* bake her butterscotch brownies and took a neat box of them along, just in case. And Lydia took along pencils and a drawing pad, but then she would probably have taken these no matter where they were going. And Kip took along his instant-developing camera. And James took along a half-worked-out idea in his mind.

Kip and Lydia led the way, because they knew where the mob-led queen lived. But as they left James and Laura's back yard, Kip suddenly smote his forehead.

"I was forgetting," he said. "Gordy!"

Lydia groaned.

"Who's Gordy?" said James.

"Gordon T. Witherspoon, Junior," said Kip.

"You mean she has *young?*" said Laura.

"Just one," said Kip. "Gordy."

"What's he like?" said James.

A discussion followed between Kip and Lydia as to whether Gordy was worse than his mother or just a little bit better. And they couldn't agree as to exactly what was so awful about Gordy, either. It wasn't that he was sissy and he wasn't downright mean, exactly.

"He's kind of white," said Kip, "and he forgets to close his mouth."

"He's got big hot wet hands," said Lydia. "I remember from that ghastly dancing school, when we were young."

"He hangs onto you," said Kip.

"He gets terrible ideas," said Lydia. "Still, maybe he won't be there."

"That's right." Kip brightened. "He's generally away. Private schools and camps. You can see why."

Laura paused as they went by the wishing well and gave it a final word. "This is the most important wish yet," she told it. "More important than the one about Miss King even. The whole future of our country depends on it. We've got to be educated."

And they set out.

Mrs. Witherspoon's stately mansion lay just down Silvermine Road, approached by way of a long curving sweep of black-top driveway. Surprisingly enough, no one stopped the four children as they went along this. An army of gardeners was visible, but each one was too busy raking and clipping and operating sprinklers to notice.

"One thing she *doesn't* need," commented Kip, "is her lawn mowed."

Mrs. Witherspoon was entertaining a friend in the garden. Her aspect as she looked up was more forbidding than usual. But the four children summoned their courage and went straight up to her.

"Would you like some butterscotch brownies?" said Laura, holding the box out. "They're scrumptious."

Mrs. Witherspoon did not take the box. "If it's Girl Scout cookies," she said, "I took six dozen just the other day, and you weren't to come back for a year!"

Laura was incensed. "It certainly isn't," she said. "*Mine* are *homemade!*"

"Well, I don't want any," said Mrs. Witherspoon, "unless it's in aid of an accredited charity. No peddlers allowed."

James pushed in front of Laura. "We're not peddling," he said. "We're making a friendly call. We think neighbors ought to be neighborly. Isn't there some little thing we could do for you? Just name it. Would you like a sketch of your house by a prize winner in the art show?"

Lydia had already put pencil to pad. But Mrs. Witherspoon made a sound that in anyone less grand might have been described as a snort.

"The idea!" she said. "My house has been painted by famous artists. You can tell that little girl to stop drawing. You won't get a penny. Not a penny."

"Oh, there's no charge," said James. "It's free. Just part of our friendly home service."

"Humph!" said Mrs. Witherspoon. "That's what they all say, at first. You don't fool me for a minute. Not a minute." She advanced toward them, glaring threateningly.

"That's fine," said Kip. "Now stop right there. Don't move. Smile." His camera clicked. Mrs. Witherspoon had not smiled. "Now if you'll just wait a second while I develop it . . ."

Mrs. Witherspoon put a hand to her forehead. "This," she said, "is persecution."

"You poor thing, does your head ache?" said Laura. "Would you like me to rub the back of your neck?"

Mrs. Witherspoon was trembling, whether with rage or fear it was difficult to say. "Don't you dare," she said. "Don't you dare. You march right off this property before I call the police."

Everybody looked at James. Even he didn't seem able to think of any more friendly home services. "I guess it's no use," he said.

"Yes," said Laura, "what's the good of being kind to somebody who won't be kind back?"

"*I* don't think she knows *how*," said Lydia.

"Why, the impudence, I never heard!" said Mrs. Witherspoon.

"I'd slap her hands!" chimed in her friend.

The four children retreated the way they had come. "You see, Adele," they heard Mrs. Witherspoon saying as they departed, "that's the way it'd be all the time. Bad, impudent children trespassing on our grounds. Juvenile delinquents. We've got to block that school."

"You're right, Florence," said her friend. "I wasn't sure before, but after what I just heard, you're right! I'm changing my vote!"

"Now see what we've done!" said James, when they were safely behind a bay of concealing shrubbery.

"We've made things worse. We've lost one of the few votes we had, even."

Everybody sat down on the grass in dejection.

"What'll we do *now?*" said Kip.

"Have some butterscotch brownies," said Laura.

There was a pause. Nobody could think of any bright ideas and besides all mouths were full. A voice broke the silence.

"What are you doing? Huh?" it said.

The four children looked up. A boy was staring at them over the top of the nearest shrub. His hair and eyelashes were light and his jaw was slack. James and Laura knew at once that it could only be Gordy.

"Can I have a cooky? Huh?" said that scion of grace and culture.

"Sure, help yourself," said Laura, passing him the box.

"Say, these are good," said Gordy explosively, through a mouthful of cooky.

James got up, dusting crumbs from his knees. "You can have what's left," he said coldly. "We're glutted." He started for the gate and the others followed.

"Where you going? Huh?" said Gordy, tagging right along. He put a hand on James's shoulder. James waited for him to take it off again, but he didn't.

"*Est-ce nécessaire que ce* goon come along *avec* us?" he muttered to the others.

"*Quel horreur!*" said Lydia.

"*Pourquoi* not?" said kind Laura.

"Sure. *Il est* harmless," said Kip.

"What you talking? French?" said Gordy.

"No, Choctaw," said James nastily. Inside he was seething. Not only was their whole day a grisly failure, but now they were saddled with this boring nincompoop. Everything was utterly and completely ruined. And they couldn't even have the satisfaction of going to the well and bawling it out or pleading with it to try harder, because the thought of letting a churl like this Gordy in on the magic was too degrading to contemplate.

"Whaddaya say we go swim in the reservoir? Whaddaya say?" said Gordy at this moment.

"Grow up, Gordy," said Lydia shortly. "With the whole river free to swim in, why do you want to go pollute the water supply?"

" 'Cause it's more fun," said Gordy simply. "Sometimes the man chases you."

James and Lydia rolled their eyes at each other. What would they do with this mindless incubus? "Whaddaya say we walk to Wilton? Whaddaya say?" growled James in bitter mockery.

But Gordy was too thick-skinned to notice when he was being made fun of. Either that, or he had got used to it. "Okay," he said, beaming toothily.

And it turned out that was what they did. Or at least they started to. James wasn't quite sure where Wilton was, but he knew it was the next town. It ought to be a good long walk, he thought to himself savagely, as he stumped along the road. Maybe Gordy would get tired and go home. Or at least it would help kill the rest of this depressing morning.

But it turned out that Gordy knew a short cut through the woods. And it turned out that he could shinny up a tree better than James and almost as well as Kip. He got dirtier than any of the rest of them, too. Maybe it was because he was so white to start out with. Black collected under his nose and among his whitish eyebrows. This ought to have made him look even worse, but somehow it didn't. Somehow it made him look more like a man and less like a mouse. Pretty soon Laura and Lydia were chatting along happily with him, almost as though he were human.

"Honestly. *Girls!*" muttered James to Kip out of the side of his mouth. "No discrimination."

But as time wore on, even James was almost beginning to get used to Gordy. Until they came on the house in the woods.

They came on it about ten minutes after they left the main road. They went over a wooded hill that was still thick with last fall's oak leaves and there it was below them, little and old and grey and forgotten. A tangle of creepers framed its door. Maple tree branches pressed against the windows as though any minute they would break in and grow right *through*. Even from a distance you could tell that nobody lived there, and that no-body *had*, for years and years. Laura broke off what she was saying, and she and Lydia and James and Kip stood gazing at the house in awe.

"Hansel and Gretel," breathed Lydia.

"Snow White," added Laura.

"Whaddaya know?" said Gordy, his voice sounding unusually loud. "I never saw that before. We must have got off the path."

"Maybe it wasn't *here* before," said Laura.

"Huh?" said Gordy.

"Maybe it's only here on special days," said Laura.

"Once every hundred years," said Kip.

"Or when special people walk by," said Lydia.

"Whaddaya mean?" said Gordy. "You talk crazy." He picked up a stone. "Whaddaya bet I can't hit one of the windows from here?"

It was then that James gave Gordy up for the second time, and completely. He didn't trust himself to say anything. He just turned his back on Gordy and walked away, thrusting his hands in his pockets for fear he would hit him.

Lydia's reaction was different. She took Gordy by both shoulders and whirled him around to face her. "What's the matter with you?" she said. "Is that all you can think of when you see a wonderful old house like that, breaking its windows?"

Gordy looked surprised. "Well? What am I *supposed* to think?"

"Don't you have any finer feelings at all?" said Lydia. "Are you just *base?* You might think all kinds of things. You might think about history, and time, and all the years it's stood there and all the people who've lived in it. You might think of poetry:

' "Is there anybody there?" said the Traveller.'

or 'The House on the Hill':

> 'They are all gone away,
> The house is shut and still,
> There is nothing more to say.' "

Gordy was sincerely baffled. "I don't get it. It's not on a hill, it's in a valley. What's so awful if I break a window? They're mostly smashed in already, anyway."

Lydia rightly ignored this. "Or," she said, "it might make you think of magic."

"Huh?" said Gordy. "Magic is for kids."

"Oh, *is* it?" said Laura, joining in. "That's all you know!"

"Yipes!" said James despairingly to Kip. "That does it. Here we go!"

Now Laura and Lydia were telling Gordy all about the well and the magic and the adventures so far, except that they left out about the mob-led queen, out of consideration for his feelings, base though they might be.

Gordy stood looking from one to another of them with his mouth open, waiting for the signal to laugh. Then it dawned on him that they might be serious.

"You crazy?" he said. "You mean it?" He saw that they did. "Okay. If you're magic, c'mon! Show me some magic tricks!"

"We can't," Laura told him. "We've got the well working on an important wish now. It's too secret to talk about. Trying to make it do anything else would distract it."

At this, Gordy's behavior sank to lower depths. Uttering a jeering laugh, he went prancing and hooting down the slope toward the house, waving his arms in a manner that James could only call asinine. The others hurried after, from some instinct to protect the house from this mindless mockery.

"Look, ma, I'm magic!" yelled Gordy. "Abracadabra! Allez-oop!" And he made an amateurish magic pass at the door of the house.

It was then that it happened.

Slowly, creakingly, the door swung inward and remained invitingly (or forbiddingly) open.

Everybody looked at everybody else.

"A quincidence?" said James.

"Or the wind," said Kip.

"Maybe it isn't," said Laura. "Maybe it's the magic still working on that wish. Maybe we're meant to go in."

"What connection could this place have?" said James. "Anyway, the magic wouldn't work through *him!* It wouldn't stoop to it."

"Maybe it would," said Laura. "You never can tell with magic. It's very democratic."

Gordy was standing rooted to the spot. His face (between the patches of dirt) looked whiter than ever. "Whaddaya say we go on home?" he said now. "Whaddaya say?"

This craven utterance awoke James's courage. "Come on," he said. He and Kip strode forward manfully into the house, and the girls and Gordy followed.

Inside all was dust and neglect and the nibble marks of squirrels. Yet the walls were covered with wonderful old paneling that was only slightly damaged, and what furniture there was standing about looked old enough to be antique at *least*. The greenery pressing against the small windows outside shut out most of the light, but as the eyes of the five children became accustomed to the darkness, Lydia suddenly gasped and pointed. "Look!"

Everyone looked.

In the dust on the floor of the hall was a footprint. It pointed away from them. Beyond it was another and another. The trail led straight across the hall and into a room on the right.

"D'you suppose we're meant to follow?" said Laura, dropping her voice to a whisper.

"What if whatever it is is still in there, *waiting* for us?" said Kip.

"It isn't," said Lydia. "It came out again. Look." Sure enough, another trail of footprints led back out of the room and across the hall to the front door.

After that they felt better. "Come on," said James. "Maybe these prints don't mean a thing. Maybe they've been there for untold ages."

"They haven't," said Lydia, always the sharpest-eyed, "or there'd be dust in them. There isn't any at all, hardly."

"It still could be last month," said James, "or last year. A year's dust would be nothing to the dust of centuries."

With bated breath the five children tiptoed across the hall and peered into the right-hand room. It was empty of people (or ghosts) and almost empty of furniture. But across the room a little old desk stood against the wall and the footsteps led straight up to it. Loud with relief, the five children raced across the room and James tried the lid. But the desk was locked. There was a keyhole but no key.

"This is maddening," said Laura. "We're *meant* to get inside. I *know* we are!"

But though they searched that room and the next one and then, growing braver, ventured upstairs and ransacked the whole house, it was a fruitless quest. Several old rusty keys turned up, but none that would fit the mysterious keyhole.

Gordy, growing ever more impossible again as he grew braver, was all for breaking in the lid, but the others stopped him.

"You *can't*," said Lydia. "It's old. It's beautiful."

"Yeah, if you like that kind of thing," said Gordy. "We've got a whole room full of 'em at home. My mom's crazy about all that stuff."

Laura was studying the desk. There were initials on the lid, in ornamental brasswork. "M.A.," she read.

"A.M., *I'd* say," said Lydia.

"They're sort of twined together so you can't tell which," said Kip.

There were some books and papers piled on top of the desk, and James started rooting among these to see whether the key were lying dormant beneath them. He picked up the top bunch of papers to move it away. Then he stood staring at what he held in his hands.

What he held in his hands was a newspaper, a *New York Times*. And it wasn't yellowed with age or musty with time, either. Its pages were crisp and white and its ink was fresh and black. It was folded to handy carrying size, as though someone had just laid it down. James looked at the date. Then he looked again.

"August 8, 1957," he said.

"That's today," said Laura, who always knew what date it was.

"Yes," said James. "It is."

He dropped the paper. There was a silence, as the eeriness of this sank in.

"Those footprints," said Kip.

"Somebody *was* just here," said Lydia.

There was another silence.

Gordy was the first to give utterance this time. What he uttered was a howl that was only half in fun.

"Wow," he said. "Lemme outa here!"

Panic, even when it's partly put on, is catching. Pretty soon it isn't put on at all any more; it's the real thing. Now prickles of fear stirred each scalp. The next instant there was a rush for the door. Pushing and jostling and tumbling into each other, the five children raced out of the house. In the open air, relief found expression in yells. They went on running across the clearing and up the woodsy slope. It was Gordy who tripped over a root and fell down.

He got up again and took a step. Then he looked surprised and his face turned white and he grabbed hold of a maple sapling. The others stopped and came back.

"It's my ankle," said Gordy. "I think I must have done something to it."

"You've cut your knee, too," said Kip, pointing to where blood welled.

"Sorry," said Gordy.

"That's all right," said James.

"You couldn't help it," said Lydia.

The cut, when examined, proved painful but not too deep. Laura bound it up with her handkerchief. A tourniquet was voted unnecessary. And now all agreed that the thing to do was get back to the main road as quickly as possible and try to hitch a ride. The trouble was that the quickest way back led past the house. But as no menacing form, ghostly or otherwise, had issued from its door and come in pursuit, there didn't seem to be anything against this.

"Silly of me to get scared," said Gordy. "Prob'ly just a tramp."

"Tramps always read the latest *New York Times*, of course," said James sarcastically.

"Maybe it was a bird watcher," said Lydia, "on a nature ramble. If we could find the house and start exploring it, somebody else perfectly respectable could, too, couldn't he? Prob'ly he's miles away by now."

But all the same, when James and Kip had made a seat of their hands and Gordy had hoisted himself onto it, the five children gave the house a wide berth and passed it in a slow procession at the farthest edge of the clearing. And everyone breathed easier when it was left behind.

Gordy, it was later agreed by all, behaved surprisingly well through the whole ordeal. Though it was plain that his knee and ankle were hurting him all the time, he tried not to wince when James and Kip jounced and jostled him. And he kept on making jokes the whole way. The jokes he made were no better than his conversation generally was; still, it was sporting of him to try.

As they went along, Laura and Lydia held a conference about the mysterious house and the locked desk.

"It must *mean* something," said Laura. "Otherwise, the magic wouldn't have led us there. Only what could it have to do with the new school? That's the wish we're *on!*"

"I don't know," said Lydia. "You never can tell with magic. Maybe it's just laughing at us."

"Do you mean," said Laura, "that it fixed things so we had to bring Gordy along and then made him fall down on *purpose?*"

"I wouldn't put it past it," said Lydia.

"Anyway," Laura consoled herself, "the way Gordy looks now, we won't have any trouble hitching a ride."

"Every time we take somebody along with us," agreed Lydia, "we seem to bring him back sort of damaged."

And in truth, Gordy at this moment did indeed resemble a refugee from a deadly invasion at *least*, with one knee in an incarnadined bandage and the other black with leaf mold. Falling down hadn't helped his dirty face either, except that under and between the dirt he was now whiter than ever with pain.

His companions looked only slightly more distinguished. Perspiration spangled Kip's brow, and James's shirttail was coming out. Lydia had torn her dress on a broken cedar branch and Laura had walked into a tangle of wild raspberry and had definitely brier-patch legs.

Altogether it was a grisly sight that confronted the general public ten minutes later when the five children burst through a final thicket of black alder and out onto the main Wilton road.

A hundred feet down the road a stately limousine was advancing toward them, headed in the direction of home. Without hesitating, Lydia stepped forward and barred the way, holding up one hand commandingly. James wished she had waited for something more modest, a Volkswagen or at most a Rambler.

The limousine swerved to avoid Lydia and at first seemed to be going to pass them by. But then a voice cried out from within.

"Can that be Gordy?" were its horrified words.

"Surely not!" said a second voice.

"It *is!* Craddock, stop the car!" cried the first voice. The chauffeur stepped on the brake, pushed the reverse button, and the car glided backwards, coming to a halt directly in front of the five children.

From its luxurious depths glared a face on which the hot flush of rage struggled with the ashen cheek of fear.

James took one look at the face. "Help!" he said. He meant it in more ways than one.

"Gordy, Gordy!" cried the owner of the face. "What have they done to you?"

Gordy smiled toothily (and a bit shakily). "Hi, Mom," he said.

A confused period followed.

There were cries of accusation and abuse from Mrs. Witherspoon and her friend (for of course it was they), interspersed with expostulations from Gordy, as the chauffeur helped him into the car. When James and Kip tried to help, too, Mrs. Witherspoon rose to new heights of fury.

"Don't you touch him!" she cried. "Bullies! Haven't you tortured the poor boy enough?"

"Aw gee, Mom, no!" said Gordy. "It wasn't like that!"

His mother brushed this aside. "Then they've led you into mischief," she said, "and that's just as bad!" She turned to her friend. "It's just as I was saying, Adele. Juvenile delinquents. Bad influences. Hooliganism."

"You're right, Florence," said her friend.

"Gee, Mom, no, you've got it wrong!" said Gordy. "They've been swell. Whaddaya say we give them a lift, too? Whaddaya say?"

"Certainly not," was what Mrs. Witherspoon said. She leaned from the car to address James and Kip and Laura and Lydia. "You are the worst children I have ever seen," she told them. "If ever I find you molesting my family or trespassing on my property again, it will mean Juvenile Court! Drive on, Craddock."

And the stately limousine glided away. The last the four children heard of it was the voice of Gordy wailing down the wind that gee, Mom, now everything was spoiled, and, "Whaddaya say we go back and apologize? Whaddaya say?"

James and Laura and Lydia and Kip were left at the side of the road, staring at each other in utter anticlimax. And they didn't even have the spirit to hail the next passing motorist but started plodding homeward in silence and on foot.

"Who'd think," said Lydia after a bit, "that she'd be right there in the first car that came along? It'd take the magic to manage a thing like that!"

"It certainly would," agreed James bitterly. "If you ask me, that magic's *black!*"

"Or else something's gone wrong with it and it's unworking," said Kip.

"Unless it's just doing it to make it harder," said ever-hopeful Laura. "So we can push on nothing daunted and prove how really noble we can be."

"What's the use?" said Lydia. "She'll be more against the school than ever now, even." And this, while not too clearly put, was all too plain to all.

"Still," said Kip, after another quarter-mile, "I don't think we ought to give up. I think we ought to do what we said before. I think we ought to talk to everybody."

"And there's still that house," said Laura. "And those footprints. I don't think the magic just put them in. I think they're supposed to *lead* us somewhere, only it's too much for our mortal minds to grasp!"

"At least we can try, I suppose," said James. But he did not sound very hopeful.

Still, for the next few days try was what they did.

That very evening they went to call on the father of the long-lost heir. He listened with interest to their problem and seemed particularly attentive when they told about finding the house in the woods. But he made no comment till the end of the story.

Then he said, "All right. If you ask me, you kids *deserve* a good school. You can count on me. I'll be there at town meeting with bells on."

The lovely movie-starish lady had come into the room in time to hear the last of the discussion.

"Oh, Gregory," she said, "are you sure you want to get mixed up in all this? We came to the country to get away from it all!"

The man looked at her. "Yes," he said. "Yes, Brenda, we did. But you can't get away from *everything*, you know. You have to get away *to* something, or where are you?"

"I think that's very true," said James approvingly.

The next day they called on Miss Isabella King.

They found her entertaining Mr. Hiram Bundy with tea and cookies. The cookies were homemade shortbread and were enjoyed by all. As Kip said, they made Lorna Doones look sick.

Miss King was indignant when she heard Laura's story.

"For shame!" she said. "I never heard of such a thing. Who *is* this Mrs. Gordon T. Witherspoon? I don't believe we've met. Some newcomer from the suburbs, I presume?"

"She's president of the Garden Club," said Kip.

Miss King sniffed. "In *my* day we felt no need of garden clubs. Our gardens *grew*. Without regimentation, to use one of your modern terms. Dear me. I have not been to town meeting in more years than I like to think. However, under the circumstances, I shall certainly attend. You have *my* vote. *And* Mr. Bundy's," she added, with a strong look at her visitor.

Mr. Bundy looked uncomfortable. "Come now, Isabella," he said. "I am to be chairman of that meeting. I must remain impartial."

"You can't," said Miss King. "On a subject like this, no one could. Surely you can say something in your speech that will help to influence people. You could wink."

"I could not," said Mr. Bundy.

"You could do *something*," said Miss King.

Mr. Bundy hemmed and hawed, but when last seen (by the four children), he seemed to be giving in.

Later that day they tackled Lydia's grandmother. She

seemed surprised that they should have thought of her.

"Are you sure you want me on your side?" she said. "No town meeting's ever agreed with me yet!"

"But you're a famous woman of America!" said Laura.

"Humph!" said old Mrs. Green. "So much the worse, if so! Just 'cause I'm an artist, they think I'm queer! I *am*, too! A plague on the pack of 'em, I say!"

Lydia was looking at her grandmother as if she were just beginning to understand her. "But you'll be there, won't you?" she said.

"If you want me," said her grandmother, "I suppose I'll have to."

After that there didn't seem to be any more important people to ask. But every day, right up to the day of the meeting, the four children spoke to any strangers they met. Some of these seemed interested, but others (probably followers of Mrs. Witherspoon) were curt and huffy.

And every night Kip's mother and father held indignation meetings with the families of other children in the school. James and Laura's parents attended these and made a lot of new friends in the town, but otherwise they didn't seem very hopeful. Mrs. Witherspoon, everyone agreed, would prevail.

"You watch," said Lydia. "She'll lead the whole mob, just the same as always."

And at last the fateful night fell.

One thing Mr. Hiram Bundy had insisted on. Since the fate of the school concerned the town's children most of all, it seemed only right that for this one town meeting the children should be there. And the authorities (after some opposition from Mrs. Witherspoon's friends) agreed.

James and Laura and Lydia and Kip and their friends and relations arrived at Town Hall early and took a place well forward on the left side of the aisle. Lydia's grandmother had accepted a ride with Laura's family, much to everyone's surprise. She did not say much, but there was a gleam in her eye.

The four children were too excited to sit still, particularly James and Laura, who had never been to a town meeting before. They kept screwing around in their seats and staring back up the aisle, watching the citizens file into the hall.

Mr. Hiram Bundy was already on the platform. He appeared nervous, particularly after Miss Isabella King made a superb entrance in an old-fashioned black lace dinner gown and swept forward to an aisle seat in the front row, where she could keep an eye on him.

The hall was beginning to fill up now, and it was interesting to see how the two factions tended to separate and sit on opposite sides. You could tell Mrs. Witherspoon's followers by their purse-proud, self-righteous expressions.

A certain stir was caused by the appearance of the

long-lost heir's father and mother and a group of their friends, all looking much more worldly and sophisticated than anyone else in the room. You could tell that they had just driven up in sports cars on their way home from cocktail parties. They were laughing as they entered the hall, but the father of the heir shushed them in disciplinary fashion. He waved at the four children and grinned, before shepherding his flock into seats on the left.

And still Mrs. Gordon T. Witherspoon was not in evidence. People were beginning to stir and mutter restlessly, and on the platform Mr. Hiram Bundy was consulting his watch for the third time.

"If that isn't just like her!" Kip's mother was heard to say. "She knows nobody'd dare to begin without her!"

From her front aisle seat Miss King gave Mr. Bundy an encouraging nod. He half rose from his chair and hesitated. Miss King nodded again, more commandingly. Mr. Bundy gave a little cough and held up his hand for silence.

And then, in a rustle of printed chiffon, Mrs. Witherspoon hurried down the aisle. Gordy followed. He was limping slightly, but appeared cheerful.

"Whaddaya say we go for a soda afterwards? Whaddaya say?" he called to the four children, just as though the whole town weren't sitting there hanging on his every word.

James didn't know what to say. He hated to ally himself with this feckless boob in front of all these people. Still, he hated to hurt Gordy's feelings, too. It wasn't his fault he came from a bad environment.

"Maybe," he answered, not meeting Gordy's eyes.

Mrs. Witherspoon's friends had saved her front-row seats, across the aisle from Miss King, and were now greeting her with nods and becks and wreathed smiles. But Mrs. Witherspoon went right past them. Her face was pink and she seemed flustered. She went straight to the edge of the platform where Mr. Hiram Bundy was standing. Mr. Bundy leaned down and they conferred together.

"Dear me," those in the front rows heard Mr. Bundy say. "It would be rather irregular."

"Be firm, Hiram!" called Miss King.

Lydia's grandmother did not agree. "Let her speak," she boomed out in her deep voice. "Have to listen to her sooner or later, anyway. Might as well get it over with!"

Mr. Bundy held up his hand for silence again. Mrs. Witherspoon turned and faced the assembly. She seemed embarrassed and reluctant, yet determined.

"I think most of you know," she began in her loud voice before which clubwomen quailed, "my feelings on the subject of this new school. I still feel that some other location would have been preferable. Somewhere in a less desirable residential district. And I certainly think the utmost care should be exercised in choosing its design; so that our beautiful countryside will not be marred by the intrusion of an eyesore! However"—and here her voice took on an aggrieved note—"my own son has recently struck up an acquaintance with certain public school children." Her eyes rested for a moment on James and Lydia and Kip and Laura, not benevolently. "And he *insists* . . ." She broke off, as if she did not like the sound of this last word.

"Go on, Mom. You're doing fine," prompted Gordy, grinning at her toothily from the front row.

Mrs. Witherspoon chose another word. "He has *decided*," she went on, "that he wishes to enroll in the public school this coming fall. Naturally where Gordy leads, others may follow. And if the trend is to be toward public education, certainly we want all the best advantages to be available. So, under the circumstances, I am forced to withdraw my objections."

"Go on," prompted Gordy again.

"And I hope all my friends will do likewise and all pull together to make our new school the best school in the county," said Mrs. Witherspoon in a rapid gabble, as though repeating a lesson. And she blushed hotly and sank into the right-hand front aisle seat.

There was a buzz in the hall that grew to a roar. Laura had an idea. She began to clap her hands. Everybody joined in the applause until Mr. Hiram Bundy had to rap for order.

James was feeling small. He had been ashamed to speak to Gordy, and all along Gordy was being a benefactor. He looked at Gordy now. Gordy typically seemed to bear no resentment. He was grinning more toothily than ever and shaking hands over his head at James, like a champion prize fighter.

Of course after Mrs. Witherspoon's speech there was hardly need to take a vote. Some of her former supporters on the right side of the aisle got up and left the building. Other die-hards remained to vote "no" as loudly as they could. It was said afterwards that Mrs. Witherspoon's friend Adele didn't speak to her for a year. But most of the people who had followed her like sheep before, just because she was Mrs. Gordon T. Witherspoon, went right on following her now that she was behaving more like a human being. The motion to build the new school on Silvermine Road was passed with an overwhelming majority.

After the meeting Mrs. Witherspoon seemed to be in a trancelike state and even allowed herself to be led to the drugstore for a soda with Gordy and the others. She answered politely when Kip's mother spoke to her and suffered in silence through a harangue by Lydia's grandmother on the subject of free education.

Just about everyone in town had crowded into the drugstore (the best one tonight, not the fairly good one nor the kidnapers' den). Miss King was there, being treated to a strawberry sundae by Mr. Bundy. She seemed to be enjoying it, though she pointed out that the ice cream was not hand-frozen nor flavored with real vanilla beans, as it would have been in *her* day.

Even the long-lost heir's father looked in for a minute with his friends to buy more cigarettes. On his way out, he stopped by the big table where Laura and Lydia and James and Kip and the others were sitting. "Congratulations," he said. "I guess you kids didn't need any help after all. Looks as if you've got your magic working again fine!"

"Say!" said Gordy, when he had gone. "Next year's going to be keen, isn't it? Whaddaya say we have magic adventures every day? Whaddaya say?"

"Whaddaya say?" echoed James weakly.

And then the drugstore began to indicate that it wanted to close.

But of course everyone was still too excited to go straight home to bed; so James and Laura's family and Lydia and her grandmother stopped off at Kip's house to talk for a while.

"I still don't understand it," said Kip's father to the four children. "You managed to fix the whole thing when none of us could think how. What did you *do?*"

"Oh, nothing," said Kip, shifting uncomfortably. He noticed that their parents were looking at them in that same peculiar way again, as if they wondered what they'd do next.

"What was all that about magic?" said the mother of

James and Laura. "Who was that man who came up to the table? Isn't he the same one who gave you those watches? Who *is* he?"

"And that wonderful old lady with Mr. Bundy," chimed in Kip's mother, "in that black dress that came out of the Ark. How did you get to know all these people?"

"It's a sort of game we've been playing," began Laura carefully, knowing that no parent could truly understand. "We call it magic because it almost seems as if it *is*, sometimes." And she told a little of what had been happening, but not much.

"Well, magic or not," said her father, "it certainly worked. Congratulations."

"Oh, that's all right," said James.

A little later, when the grownups had gone to raid the icebox and the four children were alone, he turned to the others. "You know," he said, "we've got a problem. What are we going to do about Gordy from now on?"

"Don't you sort of like him now?" said Laura. "I thought it was wonderful the way the magic's started improving him already."

"Sure, I guess it has," said James. "Sure, I guess I do. Only he seems to think now he's our best friend or something. Do we have to take him along with us on everything we do after this? Would the magic expect us to be *that* noble?"

After some discussion it was agreed by all that it would probably be all right with the magic if in future they let Gordy be their *almost* best friend and come on magic adventures with them *some* of the time, but not always.

"That's if there're any more adventures to *come* on," said Lydia. "This one felt kind of final, somehow. It was the big important wish we wanted, and the whole town sort of got in on it, and it came true. Maybe that's the end."

Laura shook her head decisively. "There's still the house in the woods," she said, "and that desk without any key. The magic wouldn't leave loose ends lying around like that. It never does. Everything's put there to add up and come out right, like the problems in arithmetic books. We just haven't figured it out yet."

"What we have to do is find the unknown quantity. Call it X," said James, who was of a mathematical turn of mind.

"No, don't," said Lydia, who wasn't.

"Anyway," said Kip, "it'll prob'ly all come out in the wish."

"Yes," said Laura. "It will. Wait and see."

There didn't seem to be anything else for them to do. But it was a long wait.

7. The Secret Drawer

Of course they had good times in the meantime. Who could help it in a fine country summer? But good times without magic do not make chapters in books, at least not in this kind of book; of course there are other kinds.

Suffice it to say that the hours did pass in one way or another, until one day it was only mid-August and the next it was suddenly almost September and Labor Day loomed ahead, and after that there would be school, only not in the new schoolhouse yet, because work on it was just barely starting. The four children often stopped by to see how it was coming, but so far all there was to see was a hole in the ground.

As for the wishing well, Laura called a wish or two down once in a while to stimulate it and let it know they hadn't lost interest, but she didn't like to make a habit of it. She had heard of wells running dry, and wasn't there a proverb about not going to the well too often?

August twenty-eighth was the day the magic finally did begin again, because Laura wrote it down in her diary later on to be remembered forever.

How they all happened to be there that day, no one could afterwards decide. It wasn't like them to go on family rides.

Yet there they were, Laura and Lydia and James and Kip squashed together in the back seat, and James and Laura's mother and father in the front with Deborah.

It was their mother who saw the sign. As their father said, she could spot them a mile off.

The sign said, "Auction Today." It was posted in front of a building called the High Ridge Community House.

James and Laura's mother clutched their father's arm. "Couldn't we?" she pleaded.

"Honestly, Margaret!" said that long-suffering man. "I thought we finally had the house all fixed up!"

"There might be bargains," murmured their mother. At that magic word, of course all resistance crumbled, and their father parked the car and they all scrambled out.

The auction was being held on the back lawn of the Community House, and the various things for sale were scattered in an abandoned-looking fashion about the grass. At one end of the lawn the auctioneer was about to deal with a bundle of sage-green plush curtains, and the mother of James and Laura hurried to get a closer look. She hated plush and had been heard to say that sage-green was an abomination unto the Lord, but to your true auction lover, the voices of good taste and common sense are as the tinkle of sounding brass.

The four children were not true auction lovers and could not have despised the sage-green curtains more; so they wandered about the lawn looking at the other things on display, in the hope of finding something more interesting.

There were the usual cut glass and hand-painted china, the usual walnut beds and scrollwork whatnots, the usual dusty books that look intriguing but turn out to be sets of John L. Stoddard's lectures and the Elsie series. There was a high chair and some battered toys and an old croquet set with a broken mallet.

Laura felt depressed, as though everyone in a family had died and his life were being laid open for the general public to peer at. Deciding she'd had enough of the auction, she let the others wander on without her and turned to go back to the car.

It was then that she saw the desk, sitting all by itself in a corner of the lawn.

She stopped short and cried out, with a note in her voice that made Lydia and James and Kip come running. Then they, too, stopped.

The four children stood in a circle, looking down at the desk. So far as they could tell, it was an exact copy of the one they'd seen in the house in the woods.

"Is it the same one, do you think?" said Lydia.

"No," said Laura. "This one's got a crack in the lid. The other one didn't."

"It's got the same initials," said James. "M.A. or A.M."

"No it hasn't," said Lydia, always observant. "This one has the M on top. The other one had the A."

"It could be a quincidence," said Kip. "They probably made hundreds of desks like these."

"Not in those days," said James. "That was before mass production. Craftsmen turned them out one by one. No two alike."

"This one's got a key in the lock," said Lydia. "Could we borrow it and see if it unlocks the other one, and then bring it back?"

"Maybe we're meant to," said James. "Maybe we were led here by unseen hands for that very purpose."

"Maybe we're meant to look inside first," said Laura. "Anyway, I'm going to."

Four hands reached out. It was Laura who turned

the key and opened the desk. Inside were what seemed to be dozens of little drawers and pigeonholes, all empty, because Laura looked and so did James and Kip and Lydia.

But in the looking, there was crowding and jostling and people's hands got in the way of other people's fingers; so that the four children couldn't tell afterwards whether someone had knocked against something or someone else had pushed something else.

However it happened, and whoever touched what, suddenly a partition that had looked solid before gave way and the secret drawer appeared.

It was probably meant to pop open when somebody touched a spring, but perhaps the wood of the desk was warped; in any event it slid only a little way out and then stuck. Nobody could be sure whether or not there was anything in it, but James afterwards swore he saw a corner of white paper.

Before anyone could pull the drawer farther open and make certain, there was an interruption.

"Really!" said a lofty voice. "This item is *sold!*"

The children turned. A tall willowy lady with long earrings was regarding them with a steely and glittering eye.

"We were just looking to see whether it's antique or not," said Laura, which was the first thing that came into her mind.

"Really!" said the lady again, more loftily than ever. "I wouldn't have a modern piece in my shop!"

"Oh, are you an antique dealer? Whereabouts?" said James, his mind racing.

"My card," said the lady, handing him a bit of pasteboard. "And now stand aside, please. Don't handle. This way, boys." And the lady bossily supervised while two workmen appeared and carted the desk away from the children's hungry gaze and into the back of the lady's station wagon.

James handed the card around for all to see. "At the Green Lantern," it read. "Luella Chippenhepple, Proprietor."

"The Green Lantern?" said Lydia. "I know where that is. Over on Route Seven."

"Mother says their prices are *exorbitant!*" said Laura.

"Do we have to *buy* it?" said Kip. "I've only got $1.13."

"I thought," said James, "we could just go over there and sort of browse. Maybe we could get a look inside the drawer."

"Or we could take a wax impression of the lock," said Kip, "like detectives in books."

"How do they do that?" said Lydia. "What kind of wax do they use?"

"I don't know," said James, "but we could study up."

"One thing we can do right now," said Laura, "is

find out where that desk came from. The auctioneer'd know."

But the auctioneer was busy right now. He continued to be busy for nearly two hours. The four children went and sat by James and Laura's mother in the front row, and didn't fidget or beg to leave the way they usually did, but waited patiently till the end.

Deborah and her father were not so patient and kept appearing from the direction of the parking lot and giving imploring looks, but the majority ruled.

When the auction was over, and James and Laura's mother was the proud possessor of a copper saucepan that needed retinning and a clock with only one hand that had stopped long ago at five minutes past some unknown hour, the four children tackled the auctioneer.

The auctioneer was old, and right now he was weary. "All this lot came from a house up in Ridgefield," he told them. "Where it was before that, I couldn't say." But when he learned which item they were interested in, his face changed. "That there desk?" he said. "That's different. I know that there desk well. It's been under my hammer time and time again. First time was back when I was a boy, learning the trade. That's how I remember. Came from Silvermine it did, when the red house was first sold up."

"The red house with the wishing well?" said Laura, breathless.

"That's right," said the auctioneer.

Everyone looked at everyone else.

"You see?" said James.

"It all connects," said Kip.

"Didn't you know it would?" said Lydia.

Next morning all was gobble and splash till breakfasts were eaten and chores done and the four children could escape and set out for Route Seven and the Green Lantern and Miss Chippenhepple and the desk. But as they issued from the gate of the red house (on bikes and Lydia's horse), another cycling figure was seen far down the road. From the way the bicycle wobbled, it could only be Gordy.

"Help!" said James.

Gordy had been coming over to see them nearly every day since the night of the town meeting. The four children usually received him with good grace and most days found themselves actually glad to see him. But today, somehow, the thought of him was too much.

"We said he didn't have to be in on everything, didn't we?" said Lydia.

"Let's hide," said Kip. And all, even tender-hearted Laura, agreed. Bikes were propped against the fence, the horse hastily tied to a tree, and the four children dashed for the woods.

They were hardly in time. Gordy biked into the yard just as Laura, the slowest runner, flopped down behind a spicebush.

He looked around at horse and bikes and called their names a few times. In the woods, nobody said anything. Nobody looked at anybody else, either. Gordy hesitated, puzzled, seemed about to wait, got off his bike, then finally got on it again and slowly pedaled away.

The four children came out of hiding. By now everyone was feeling sorry, the way you always do, but still no one talked about it. The long ride to Route Seven was accomplished almost in silence.

The Green Lantern, when they arrived, looked every bit as fussy and expensive as they had known it would. As they hesitated before its entrance, the door opened and two workmen issued forth. They were carrying the desk. Miss Chippenhepple followed, bossing them fussily.

James found his tongue. "That desk," he said.

"Sold," said Miss Chippenhepple.

"Who to?" said Lydia ungrammatically.

Miss Chippenhepple's voice took on a note of pride. "As a matter of fact," she said, "I picked it up for Mrs. Gordon T. Witherspoon. And now, was there anything special? Because I am about to close the shop and deliver it personally."

Four silent heads shook. Once again the desk was loaded in Miss Chippenhepple's station wagon and she drove away.

"Mrs. Witherspoon," said Laura. "It all keeps connecting."

"Of course that settles it," said Lydia. "We'll have to let Gordy in on it now."

"Sure," said James. "That's why the magic did it this way. It's paying us back and we deserve it."

"Yes," said Kip. "We're supposed to do good turns, and hiding from Gordy was the opposite."

Everyone grew weary on the long uphill-and-down-dale ride home, but none complained. And hardly had they reached Silvermine Road when they met Gordy himself, biking down to see *them* again. He beamed at them in utter friendliness, as usual. If he suspected their base behavior, he did not mention it.

But he seemed less excited than they had been when he heard what had happened, maybe because he hadn't had so much experience of the magic as they had.

"Your old desk's prob'ly at the house now," he told them. "That Miss Chippenhepple was just driving up when I came away."

"What are we waiting for?" said James. "Let's go take a look."

"Sure," said Gordy. "There's just one thing. Mom."

"You mean she still doesn't like us," said Lydia.

"I wouldn't say *that*," said Gordy. "I've told her what swell kids you are. But I think we ought to let her get used to the idea awhile. I don't think she ought to actually *see* you just yet. Whaddaya say we wait till the coast is clear? Whaddaya say?"

Everyone agreed to approach Mrs. Witherspoon's house with utter caution.

But as they came stealthily around the last curve of the driveway a few minutes later, a loud voice and an uppity one were heard from the direction of the rock garden.

"It's all right," said Gordy. "She's showing that Miss Chippenhepple her creeping palsy, or whatever the latest plant is."

"Crawling rabbitbane," said Laura to Lydia.

" 'Manypeeplia Upsidownia,' " said Kip.

Everybody giggled.

"Shush," said James.

They entered the house in silence and followed Gordy into a room on the right of the hall that was the Antiques Room, he told them.

It certainly lived up to its name. It looked more like part of a museum than a room people were supposed to live in. Highboys and lowboys and Dutch cupboards and hutch cupboards lined its walls. Little tables of all sorts were dotted about its middle. There were chairs here and there, but most of these had velvet ropes strung from arm to arm; so that no one would forget himself and sit in one of them.

The four children paid small heed to any of these, because there against the far wall was the desk, sitting by itself in a cleared space as though it were on display. They went up to it.

"Hurry!" said Laura, who was nervous in Mrs. Witherspoon's house. "Let's borrow the key and go see if it fits the lock of the other desk now."

Maybe if they had done that, the story might have ended differently.

But "No," said James. "I think we're supposed to look in the secret drawer first. Otherwise, why did the magic show it to us?"

Everyone thought he knew just where the secret drawer had been. As before, four hands reached out. This time Gordy's hand reached out, too, for who could resist trying to be the one who finds and presses the spring?

Five minutes later everyone was still trying. The drawer still remained stubbornly concealed. Tempers were getting cross and voices were getting louder.

"My hand was on this panel before," said Lydia, "and I think it kind of slid."

"*I* just closed this drawer," said Kip, "and I think that did it."

"Get out of the way," said James succinctly (and rudely), pushing his hand between theirs to shove at a bit of ornamental carving.

The delicate desk fairly vibrated under their combined probing.

With part of her mind Laura thought she heard the sound of a car driving away. But she was too busy twisting at the knob of one of the drawers to let the impres-

sion sink in. She was sure this was what she'd been doing before.

Still, maybe it was the memory of what she had half
heard that made her look up a moment later and glance
at the doorway.

The others looked up only a second after Laura did.
Their voices broke off. Mrs. Gordon T. Witherspoon
was standing in the entrance of the room regarding
them.

At first Laura didn't think she looked so cross as
usual. But then she wondered how she could have
thought this, for now Mrs. Witherspoon was frowning
in awful majesty and her voice, when she spoke, was
terrible.

"Gordy!" was all she said. It was enough.

"Hi, Mom," said Gordy sheepishly. "You know
everybody here, don't you?"

"Yes," said Mrs. Witherspoon, not sounding a bit
glad of it, "I do. Gordy, what are you thinking of?" she
went on. "You know you are never to play in this
room! The idea, mistreating my lovely new early Vic-
torian desk! Tell your friends good-by this minute.
Outdoors," she added threateningly.

The four children slunk past Mrs. Witherspoon and
out the front door. Laura did not dare to ask now if
they might borrow the key.

But once in the front yard Gordy appeared quite
cheerful.

"Sorry," he said. "She still isn't used to the idea of you yet."

"We noticed," said Lydia.

"It'll be all right, though," said Gordy. "I think she's going out to dinner tonight. I'll phone you when it's safe to come back."

"Better not make it too late," said James dubiously. "We can't always get away after dark."

"Oh, do you let them order you around?" said Gordy. "I never do."

The others treated this idle boasting with the silent contempt it deserved. The thought of not letting yourself be ordered around by Mrs. Witherspoon was too absurd to contemplate.

"No peeking inside," warned James sternly, "till we're all here."

"Scout's honor," promised Gordy solemnly. Then he went in.

This solution wasn't very satisfactory to the four children. Still, no other seemed to offer itself; so they all trailed back to James and Laura's house and waited to see what would develop.

They waited and waited, through lunch and all afternoon.

Lydia and Kip hung about long after James and Laura's father came home and dinner noises began in the kitchen and politeness counseled them to leave. And then finally they *did* leave and were late getting home to their own dinners, and still there was no word from Gordy. The telephone had kept ringing all afternoon, but always it was for James and Laura's mother.

After dinner it started getting dark fast, for the days were beginning to close in. James and Laura sat looking out as dusk turned to night and the moon shone down.

It was nearly nine o'clock when the call came at last. James got to the telephone first, but he held the receiver out so Laura could hear, too.

"It's okay," came the voice of Gordy. "Hurry up. Hoot like an owl four times and wait till the lone wolf howls."

"We'll try," said James doubtfully.

But to their surprise, their parents made no objection when they asked if they could walk down to Gordy's house.

"After all, it's a moonlight night," said their father.

"Don't be *too* late," said their mother.

It was the same at Kip's house.

As for Lydia's grandmother, of course she hardly knew whether Lydia came or went when she was painting a picture or planning the next one, which was what she was doing now.

The four children met in the road. Kip had brought along a flashlight, but Lydia made him turn it off; so it would be more mysterious. The moon just then chose to go behind a cloud and Lydia repented. But wild horses would not have made her say so.

Even when the moon came out again, the road looked strange, as country roads do at night. Near things seemed nearer and far things farther. The bushes that screened Mrs. Witherspoon's grounds were spooky. When Kip hooted like an owl, it did not make them seem any less so. Laura and Lydia huddled close together.

But the lone-wolf howl that followed sounded so exactly like Gordy in its rather bleating tones that the delicious terror evaporated and everybody laughed. It was a friendly laugh, though. Good old Gordy, it said.

Good old Gordy was waiting for them in the open front door as they came up to the house. They all turned right into the Antiques Room. This time there was no pushing and jostling. Under James's direction, all five children took hold of the lid of the desk at once and opened it carefully.

And this time there was no vain search for the secret drawer. The secret drawer was already ajar. In the crack that showed, an edge of whitish paper could be seen.

"Somebody must have touched the spring after all, before," said Kip.

The drawer still seemed to be stuck and wouldn't come out any farther, but James was able to catch hold of the edge of the paper and drew it out gently, for it was old and stiff and the edges were yellowed and crumbly.

Then he seemed to stop and think. "*You* read it," he said, and handed it to Gordy. That was to make up for a lot of things.

Gordy seemed fully sensible of the honor. Lydia thought that he blushed. He opened the paper's crackly folds and looked. Then, "It's all faded," he said. "I can't make it out. *You* read it." And he handed it back. Let James be the leader. He was content to follow.

James looked at the paper and its faded, old-fashioned copperplate handwriting. "It says 'Eternal Friendship,' " he said, "with a kind of garland around it. And a date, '1850.' And then there're two signatures. 'Mehitabel Anne King. Anne Mehitabel King.' "

"M.A.," breathed Laura triumphantly, "and A.M.! Like on the two desks," she added, as if anyone needed to be told.

"King," said Kip. "Any relation to Miss Isabella, I wonder?"

"And then down below there's another date," said James. "Eighteen ninety-one. Forty years later. And a kind of poem." His eye traveled down the page. "I don't think it's very good."

"Never mind that," commanded Lydia. "Read on. Out loud. No skipping ahead."

James read the poem.

> " 'Alas, that one of two should roam
> Afar from friendship's childhood home!

Let him who finds, in friendship's name,
Restore the truant whence it came.
And he who makes these twain be one,
If it be done by light of sun,
I wish him joy upon the well
From joyless Anne Mehitabel.
But if it be by shine of moon,
Then he may gain a special boon:
My ghost shall grant his wish entire
And he shall have his heart's desire.' "

"Clear as mud," said Lydia.

"What does it mean?" said Kip.

"It's very simple," said James. "There were these two girls and they had these two desks. Then I guess one of them moved away and took her desk with her. Then afterwards I guess she was sorry."

"And her ghost goes on worrying about an old desk?" said Lydia. "Before I'd be so paltry if I were a ghost!"

"I think there's more to it than that," said Laura. "I think it's a kind of symbol. It says about the wishing well, too! It all goes right on connecting!"

"What are we supposed to do next?" said Kip.

"Take this desk back to the other one, of course," said James. " 'Restore the truant whence it came,' it says."

"How do we know it came from there?" said Lydia. "If this desk's been sold around a lot of places, the other one could have been, too."

"I don't think that matters," said James. " 'Make these twain be one,' it says. That's the important thing. So we move this desk down to the house in the woods. Then we get a wish."

"Better than that," said Lydia. "It's moonlight out," she reminded them. " 'But if it be by shine of moon . . . !' Our 'heart's desire,' it says!"

"Gee," muttered Kip. "I wonder what my heart's desire *is*. I never thought."

"But we can't just take Mrs. Witherspoon's desk," said Laura. "It would be stealing."

"Oh, that," said Gordy. "That's all right. I'll explain to Mom. She'll understand."

Laura wondered if she would. It didn't seem very like her.

"How'll we get it there?" said Kip.

"There's my horse," said Lydia. "Does anyone have a buggy?"

Nobody had.

"Deborah's wagon!" James cried suddenly. All agreed that this was an inspiration.

James went out the door with Kip after him. Neither one gave a thought to the spookiness of the road this time. They had too much on their minds. James's only concern was whether his parents would hear him taking the wagon from the garage.

But he needn't have worried. "Home already, dear?" his mother called from a window.

"We just want to borrow Deborah's wagon for a minute," James said, wondering what he'd say when his mother asked him why.

But "Very well, dear," was all she said. James couldn't understand it, unless the magic were beginning to operate already.

The two boys felt silly, pulling a kid's wagon down the road in the moonlight, but they felt even sillier on the second lap of the trip. Gordy and the girls had moved the desk onto the front stoop, and to get it from there to the wagon was the work of but a moment. And no faithful servants heard and came to the defense of Mrs. Witherspoon's property, either.

But the desk was too big to fit *in* the wagon and had to be turned on its side (carefully out of regard for its fragile antiquity) and lashed in place with some rope Gordy found in the basement.

This made rather a top-heavy wagon to pull, and someone had to keep running along on each side of it and bending over to steady it from tipping, which was difficult enough on Silvermine Road, but on the trafficky route to Wilton it was maddening. Kind grownups kept stopping to ask what they were doing and if they needed any help, and rude teen-agers made jeering remarks.

All in all it was a relief when they came to the spot where the short cut turned off through the woods. Only now they had to abandon the wagon and edge the

desk along by hand. The boys spelled each other at this, two hauling while the third went ahead to clear the way of clutching branches. Beech branches were the worst. The procession moved slowly uphill, stumbling over rocks and stones and trees. Luckily the desk escaped serious mishap.

Luckily too Kip still had his flashlight and Lydia played this upon the scene. But as they drew near the house in the woods, Laura made her switch it off. The poem had specified moonlight and Laura felt that it should be unadulterated.

And now all idle chatter broke off, and they covered the last climb in silvered silence. Kip and James and Gordy maneuvered the desk through the narrow doorway. Inside it was darker, for the small old-fashioned windows of the house let in only a few random moonbeams. The five children stopped for a minute to rest and catch their breaths. There was a new feeling in the air, a kind of solemnity.

Gently James and Kip moved the desk into the inner room and set it down next to the other.

Laura stepped forward. She altered the position of the desks a little; so that the moonbeams from the window above fell on both of them. She unlocked Mrs. Witherspoon's desk and opened the lid. Somehow it seemed to be the thing to do. Then she tried the key in the lock of the other. It fitted and turned, just as she had known it would. She opened the second desk and moved away.

The five children stood looking at the two desks shining in the moonlight.

There was a step on the stair.

8. Magic or Not?

For a long minute no one dared to look.

Then, slowly, all heads turned.

The person who stood on the stairway, where it came down into the room, was in darkness, but a slanting ray of moonshine showed her hooped skirt. Her face was in shadow, but the moon glinted on her dark hair.

James was the first to find his voice.

"Are you Anne Mehitabel or Mehitabel Anne?" he asked huskily.

"I am Anne Mehitabel," said the person (if it was a

person). Her voice was faint and yet clear, sweet and yet ringing, as one might expect of a ghost.

"Were you sisters?" said Lydia.

"Cousins," said the ghost (if it was a ghost), "but brought up together, closer than sisters, for a time."

"And then something happened," guessed Laura.

"A misfortune," said the presence (whatever it was). "There was trouble. A quarrel about money."

"That's always the worst kind of quarrel there is, Pop says," said Kip. " 'Specially between relatives."

"Your father says rightly," said the figure. "It was indeed the very worst kind of quarrel. And then I went away and we never spoke again, though I lived so very near, in the red house with the wishing well."

"Where we live now," said Laura. "Couldn't you have said you were sorry and made it up?"

"By the time I was sorry, too long a time had gone by and I was too proud. Once she came to my door and I would not answer. That was the worst thing. And then, sooner than you would believe, we were old. They said I grew queer then. Some shunned me for a witch. But some came to me. They said I had magic power. They believed the things I wished on the well came true. Perhaps it was so. Perhaps I helped them. But magic or not, I could never use my power to help myself. The one wish I made over and over again . . . that I would forget my pride . . . that never came true."

"The well's still like that," Kip told her. "The wishes we made for ourselves never panned out."

"It still works fine for good turns, though," said Lydia. "We've been using it all summer."

"That's how we found the desk," said James, "and got your message."

"Or maybe you already knew that," said Laura. "Maybe it was you leading us on, all along?"

"Perhaps it was, in a way," said the voice from the staircase. "Just before I died, I came upon the old drawing of Friendship's Garland that Mehitabel and I had made. And I wrote the rhyme and made my last wish on the well. I wished that in time to come someone new would chance on the power of the well and use its magic until at last the spell of my old selfishness would be broken and the lost would be found and the wrong I did would be undone. And now that it has happened, perhaps Mehitabel Anne's ghost will forgive mine."

"I still don't understand why you cared about bringing that old desk back," said Lydia. "I don't see where it enters in."

"Open the secret drawer," said the voice. "All the way."

"We can't," said Kip. "It's stuck."

"Force it," said the voice.

James took hold of the edge of the drawer and pulled. Suddenly it shot forward. The others crowded round to see. There was a packet inside that had got jammed against the roof of the drawer. That was why the drawer wouldn't come all the way out before.

"Open it when I am gone," said the voice, "and you will know the answer."

"Is the magic in the well finished now?" said Laura. She couldn't bear to think that it was.

"The spell *I* put upon it has run its course," said the voice from the staircase, "but you never can tell with wells. Sometimes they renew themselves. Some of the magic from the good turns you did may have leaked back into it. It might start it up again any day."

"Like priming a pump." James nodded sagely.

"What about the last wish?" Gordy spoke for the first time. "It's shine of moon out. What about the heart's desire?"

Everyone glared at him, to show they thought this was terribly crude and in bad taste. Still, reasoned Laura, why was it? After all, wasn't it what they all were thinking? Gordy might not have much delicacy, but he certainly got to the point.

"Open the other secret drawer," said the voice. "Read what you will find and see if it merits the description."

The four children ran to the second desk. There was no trouble finding the secret drawer this time, for they all knew where it should be and it opened easily at the first touch. There was a paper inside with four names on it, James and Laura and Lydia and Kip, in the same faded copperplate handwriting as in the Friendship's Garland poem. James took up the paper, but before he could open it, something made them all turn again toward the stairway.

The figure was gone.

The four children (and Gordy) rushed to the foot of the stairs. They were in time to see a curious thing.

In the faint glimmer of moonlight they could just make out the dim figure of the lady climbing the stair. And as she neared the top, another identical figure appeared, moving toward her. For an instant the two ghostly forms seemed to merge. Then all was blackness.

"Mehitabel Anne forgave her," breathed Laura.

No one ventured a foot on the stair. All five, even Gordy, knew when a thing was finished and when not to inquire further.

Laura and Lydia and James and Kip moved back to the brightest patch of moonlight. James opened the folded paper.

"Wasn't it smart of the magic to figure out what our heart's desire really was?" said James next afternoon, as the four children and Gordy were assembled in the front yard of the red house. "And here all along I thought what I wanted was a tape recorder."

"*I* thought I wanted a course at the Art Students

League," said Lydia. "But I guess that can come later. What we did get is dandy for now."

"The house in the woods to belong to the four of us forever, for our very own," breathed Laura as though she still couldn't believe it and had to keep repeating it to remind herself. "Who could ask for anything more?"

"If the magic starts up again, it can be our secret witch's hut where we do our good-turn sorcery," said Lydia.

"And if it doesn't, it'll make a dandy clubhouse," said James.

Kip hadn't said anything. "What's the matter?" Lydia asked him. "Wasn't it your heart's desire, too?"

"Oh, sure," said Kip. "I guess it'd be just about anybody's." But he seemed pensive.

"The most wonderful thing," said Laura, "is that money that was jammed in the drawer of the other desk all these years. That money that Anne Mehitabel took away with her, all that long time ago."

"She certainly went the long way round, returning it," said James.

"But it worked out just in time," said Laura, gloating over the happy ending. "Now Miss Isabella's the last surviving member of the family and it'll all come to her and she'll never have to worry any more."

"I didn't think she'd have to, anyway," said Lydia. "I thought she'd prob'ly marry Mr. Hiram Bundy any day now and live in the lap of luxury."

"I don't think she wants to," said Laura. "I don't think he does, either. I think they'd both rather go on the way they are, with him coming to tea and her bossing him around. I think they're set in their ways. And now they can *stay* set."

"The only thing that bothers me," said James, "is about the heart's desire thing. The paper *said* the house in the woods belongs to us now, but how could the magic go giving things away like that? There're laws about property!"

Kip stood up. "I know," he said. "That's it. That worried me, too. That's why I went to Town Hall this morning and looked up the deed."

"Well?" said Laura.

"Well," said Kip, almost unwillingly, "it used to belong to the King family, way back. That part of it's fine."

"Sure," said Lydia. "That's prob'ly how the desk happened to be there in the first place."

"All right," said Kip, "but it's been sold a lot of times since. And you know who owns it now? The lost heir's father!" He let this sink in.

"You mean . . . ?" began Laura, and stopped.

"He could have been there that first day," said James, "inspecting his property."

"He's prob'ly the one who left that *New York Times*," said Lydia. "He prob'ly heard us come in, and everything we said."

Kip nodded. "And you know what? I found out all about him. That wife of his is an actress."

"She is?" said Laura, as a dread possibility occurred to all.

"And you know what else?" went on Kip. "I biked over there this morning and looked. There's a full-length mirror at the top of those stairs!"

"You mean it was all just somebody playing a part?" said James. "You mean it was all done with mirrors, there at the end? What would be the point?"

"Humoring the dear little children with their magic games!" said Kip bitterly.

"But she never even seemed to *like* us," wailed Laura. "She wouldn't be bothered, doing all that!"

"Imagine learning all those lines!" said Lydia.

"She'd have done it if he told her to," said Kip.

"But that would mean . . ." said James. He stopped at the thought of all that it would mean.

"Start figuring from the beginning," said Kip. "That's what *I* did. Say the heir's father *was* in the house somewhere and heard us. He knew we thought the first desk was magic."

"But *nobody* could have known we'd find the second desk at the auction," said Laura.

"*He* might have," said Kip unhappily, and yet seeming to enjoy it, too, in a way. "He might have stopped at the auction to look around, just the way we did. And then he saw the desk and realized it was like the other one, and that gave him the idea."

"Then he'd have to have written that poem," said Laura, "and put it in the desk right there."

"Or—no! You know what I think?" said James excitedly. "I don't think that poem was even *in* the desk then!" He turned on Gordy. "We didn't see it till later, at *your* house, and then it was sticking right out! Did the heir's father come to your house that day?"

Gordy's face was toothily honest as he shook his head solemnly. "No, we don't even know him. *Nobody* came."

Lydia was staring at Gordy now. "*You,*" she breathed. "*You* were there with that desk the whole afternoon! While we waited and waited! No wonder it took so long! You could have been making up that poem then!"

"*Me?*" said Gordy, his voice going up high and bleating. "Whaddaya think I am? I couldn't even rhyme two lines!"

"Then your mother . . ." began Lydia. Then even she broke off. The thought of Mrs. Gordon T. Witherspoon's going to the effort of getting old yellowed paper and faded ink and making up a poem and writing it out in imitation copperplate handwriting, for the benefit of any child but her own, seemed too absurd to contemplate.

"Why, *everybody* would have had to be in on it,

when you come to think," said Laura. "Our parents and everybody! Otherwise, how could anyone be sure we'd stop at the auction and see the other desk?"

"Start at the beginning again," said James. "The heir's father could have been in the house in the woods that day. Maybe he wanted to give us more of a reward, besides the watches. He knew about the magic. He could have told our parents and Mrs. Witherspoon and everybody! Maybe even the auctioneer! He could have had both desks and put the other one in the auction just so we'd see it!"

"Don't!" wailed Laura. "I don't want to hear about it. And even if all that were true, what about Miss King's money? And Anne Mehitabel?"

"That's if there ever *was* an Anne Mehitabel," said Lydia.

"Well, yes, there was," admitted Kip, "and a Mehitabel Anne, too. I looked *them* up in the town records, too."

"Well, then?" said Laura. "*Nobody* could have arranged all that."

"That old, *old*-looking money," said Lydia.

"There're ways of making money *look* old," said James. "Miss Isabella's a deserving case. Everybody's been wondering how to take care of her. If Kip could look up old Mehitabels in the town records, so could anyone else. The whole town might have clubbed together!"

"Mr. Hiram Bundy," said Kip.

"Probably the Chamber of Commerce," said Lydia bitterly.

"Why," said Laura, "it'd have to have been the biggest conspiracy since Aaron Burr!" Then her square jaw suddenly looked even squarer and she shook her head. "No," she said. "No, it's too much. And anyway, what about the good deeds all summer? And the wishes that worked out? *They* were magic all right. And if one part was magic, it stands to reason the whole thing must have been. And that's what I'm going to believe."

James's face brightened. "Besides," he said, "suppose it *was* a conspiracy. Think of all those people who didn't even know each other. It'd take magic to make them all get together and work out a thing like that in the first place!"

There was a pause, as the good sense of this sank in. Kip's troubled frown smoothed itself out. Laura relaxed. Lydia began to smile.

"Well, magic or not," she said, "it's been a wonderful summer."

"It certainly has," said Kip.

"I didn't know I *could* have a good time like this," said Gordy rather shyly, as though he didn't want to push himself forward but he had to speak out.

"Oh, nonsense," said Laura idly. "You must have had lots of good times and lots of friends, at all those different schools you've gone to."

She was sorry afterwards she'd said it, for a peculiar expression came over Gordy's face. He looked away and dug a bare toe in the earth. Then he looked back at her. "Oh, not so many," he said.

There was another silence.

"I wonder if the well's still magic," said Lydia.

"No," said Laura, "it isn't. I tried this morning. It was a good turn, too. I was brushing Deborah's hair and I wished she'd be cured of all those cowlicks. But it was snarlier than ever."

"Oh well," said James, "maybe the pump just isn't primed enough yet. Maybe it'll decide to renew itself some other day. Right now I'm willing to take time out." He yawned and stretched out on the grass in the sun.

Everyone else felt the same, contented and lazy and willing to lie back and rest up from the magic for a long time, maybe even till next summer.

Then suddenly Lydia sat up indignantly.

"I just thought," she said. "Gordy! You should have had a wish last night, too, with the rest of us! You didn't get any heart's desire at all!"

The same peculiar expression came over Gordy's face. He looked away and dug his toe into the earth again. Then he beamed around at them all toothily (and lovingly).

"I guess I already had it," he said.